Mystery at Moorsea Manor

Nancy pressed the accelerator of the small silver-colored sedan, guiding it onto the right-hand fork. After she took the turn, the road suddenly narrowed.

"Weird," she commented, eyeing the high privet hedge that was now inches from her window. "If this is the main road, I'd hate to see what the other road is like."

"We'd have been squished, for sure," George said.

The road veered sharply left. Nancy swung the steering wheel hard. With its wheels squealing, the car followed the curve.

Nancy's eyes widened in disbelief: She was heading up the steepest hill she'd ever driven on. The car appeared to shoot straight into the air, at what seemed to be a ninety-degree angle, although Nancy realized that would be impossible. Are we going to flip over backward? she wondered.

The car skidded. Nancy caught her breath, her thoughts racing. If these wheels can't get traction, she realized, the car will slip backward—all the way down the long, steep hil

Nancy Drew
Mystery Stories

Available from MINSTREL Books

NANCY DREW® 150

MYSTERY AT MOORSEA MANOR

CAROLYN KEENE

A MINSTREL® BOOK

Published by POCKET BOOKS
New York   London   Toronto   Sydney   Tokyo   Singapore

This book is a work of fiction. Names, characters, places and incidents are products of the author's imagination or are used fictitiously. Any resemblance to actual events or locales or persons living or dead is entirely coincidental.

A MINSTREL PAPERBACK *Original*

 A Minstrel Book published by
POCKET BOOKS, a division of Simon & Schuster Inc.
1230 Avenue of the Americas, New York, NY 10020

ISBN: 0-671-02787-5

First Minstrel Books printing July 1999

10 9 8 7 6 5 4 3 2 1

Cover art by Ernie Norcia

Printed in the U.S.A.

Contents

MYSTERY AT
MOORSEA MANOR

1

Too Steep to Handle

George Fayne woke up with a start as her friend Nancy Drew slowed the car. "Are we there yet?" George asked hopefully. "I mean, it's been hours since we left Heathrow Airport."

Eighteen-year-old Nancy rounded a curve in the narrow road, then shot George a quick grin. "How would you know how long it's been? You've been sleeping the whole time."

George yawned, then peered impatiently out the window at the steep green hills rushing by. "Give me a break, Drew. After that marathon flight from Chicago to London, I'm allowed some shut-eye." She paused, then added, "Anyway, it seems like this whole trip has taken forever. I can't wait to see Moorsea Manor."

1

Nancy smiled. "I'm eager to get there, too. From Aunt Eloise's description, the place sounds awesome—a luxury inn on a four-hundred-acre sheep farm with tennis courts and four-star cooking. The Petersons grow all their own vegetables and herbs. And the picture in Aunt Eloise's brochure shows a cool-looking gray-stone manor house on a bluff above the sea."

"I guess that's why the place is called Moorsea," George broke in. "Because it's between the sea and the moors."

"Uh-huh," Nancy said. "It's between the English Channel and Dartmoor, the largest national park in Devonshire. Dartmoor is supposed to have some great places to hike, and even though Moorsea isn't actually in Dartmoor, you can ride or hike to nearby moors. Dartmoor has kind of a creepy reputation. There are a ton of ghost stories about it. Lots of mysterious things seem to happen there."

George frowned skeptically. "I guess that Sherlock Holmes story, *The Hound of the Baskervilles*, did take place there, didn't it?" She shrugged, then continued, "Anyway, everyone was super impressed when I told them where we're staying. The man I sat next to on the plane told me there's a real buzz going on about Moorsea in London. He said it's *the* cool place to weekend."

Nancy nodded, remembering the conversation.

"Moorsea Manor is incredibly popular. Aunt Eloise made her reservation to stay there months ahead of time."

"I feel bad for your aunt Eloise," George went on, sitting up straight. "She must have been so disappointed when she sprained her ankle and had to cancel at the last minute."

"You're not kidding," Nancy agreed. "But she was glad we could take her place on short notice. And I'm glad, too. I'm really up for a vacation."

"Ditto," George said, with a toss of her short dark hair. Then she flashed Nancy a knowing smile. "Let's hope it really is a vacation, if you know what I mean, Nan."

Nancy laughed. "I think I can guess," she said slyly. Though she was still a teenager, Nancy was already an accomplished detective. George and Bess Marvin, Nancy's other best friend and George's cousin, often helped Nancy solve mysteries that had stumped much older detectives.

"It's just that wherever you go, Nan, a mystery usually follows," George added with a grin.

Nancy's blue eyes sparkled. "I promise you, George, that I'll do my best this time to have a mystery-free vacation."

Rolling her eyes, George said, "Yeah, right. It's too bad Bess couldn't join us. She might have helped me keep you in line."

At that moment Nancy caught sight of a wide expanse of blue glittering in the distance. Tiny

3

white patches constantly appeared, then disappeared, on the the smooth surface. "Look, George," she said, "there's the sea—with white-caps even. We might be able to take a boat out once we get to Moorsea. I'll bet there's a good wind today."

"Super!" George exclaimed happily. "Do you think they'll have other sports besides tennis and boating?"

Nancy grinned. Typical George, she thought—always thinking about sports. "Let me see," she answered. "Well, there's riding, hiking, croquet, biking—you name it. When Annabel and Hugh Peterson turned their manor house into an inn, they went all out. That's why it's got such an awesome reputation."

"What else did your aunt Eloise tell you about Moorsea?" George asked curiously. "Didn't you say she had a friend in common with the Petersons who gave her the lowdown on it?"

"That's right," Nancy said, gripping the steering wheel tightly as she negotiated another hairpin curve. "According to Aunt Eloise's friend, Annabel inherited Moorsea from her parents, Colonel and Mrs. Trevellyan, five years ago when they died. It has been in Colonel Trevellyan's family since the seventeen hundreds."

"Wow. And to think the Fayne estate has been in the family since the nineteen hundreds," George quipped.

4

Nancy smiled. "Some places in England have been owned by the same family for even longer than Moorsea has." She pushed a lock of her shoulder-length reddish blond hair behind an ear and stole a quick look at George. "But Annabel almost lost Moorsea," she continued. "After her parents died, she had to settle all the debts and inheritance taxes. She was really strapped for cash and couldn't pay the taxes on the place."

George let out a low whistle. "I'll bet the real estate taxes on four hundred acres are astronomical."

"I'm sure they're enormous," Nancy replied. She glanced out the window at endless green hills dotted with rocks and high granite outcroppings. Every now and then patches of forest, dark and forbidding even in the bright afternoon sun, would flash by, nestled in valleys or alongside hills. Nancy shivered, remembering the tales she had heard about nearby Dartmoor—its ghosts—and also about the dangerous thieves and smugglers who had roamed the Devonshire coast years ago.

A sudden bend in the road caught Nancy by surprise. With a quick turn of the steering wheel, she managed to keep the car in control as she rounded the curve. "Whew," she said, "these roads aren't easy. Especially since I'm not used to driving on the left-hand side."

"I keep wanting you to move over to the right, like in the States," George said, "but then, of course, we'd hit another car."

Nancy smiled. "Luckily, the roads seem pretty empty, but I'll do my best not to hit another car, George, and to remember to stay on the left. Anyway, the Petersons loved Moorsea Manor," she went on, "and they were desperate to keep it. The thought of her childhood home being sold off to raise taxes practically killed Annabel. So the Petersons came up with this plan—they used the rest of Annabel's inheritance to turn Moorsea Manor into a money-making luxury inn."

"Well, it sounds like they succeeded," George said. "If it's as popular as everyone says, they must be making a fortune on it."

"I don't know about *that*," Nancy said, pursing her lips. "I'm sure most of the money they make gets poured back into the inn. The Petersons raise all those sheep, and they even make their own cheese and process wool right on the farm. They've got stables, vegetable and flower gardens, first-class accommodations, and a fabulous restaurant. It must cost them a fortune to run."

"True, but I'm sure they're operating in the black or else they'd have lost Moorsea by now," George reasoned.

Nancy nodded in agreement, then added, "But the Petersons aren't running the business just for the money. I've heard they love being innkeep-

6

ers. In fact, what makes Moorsea so special for visitors isn't just the amazing setting and the luxury. It's the Petersons as hosts."

"What's so special about them?" George asked.

"They're supposed to be friendly and warm and also incredibly stylish and fun," Nancy told her. "Apparently, the Petersons have this knack for making guests feel as if they're totally special, as if they've all been invited to a private house party."

As Nancy spoke, the narrow road, which was now running between two enormous privet hedges that blocked all views, suddenly widened into a fork. Nancy paused and peered at a sign up ahead that was on the right-hand side of the fork.

"Hmm," George said, squinting into the sunlight. "That sign says 'A Road, Avoiding the Ramsgate Hill.' But the road to the left is unmarked."

Nancy leaned forward. "Not totally," she said, pointing to the left-hand side of the fork. "See that hole in the ground? It looks like there could have been a sign there."

"You're right," George said. "I wonder what happened to it."

"Me, too," Nancy said, then shrugged. "Well, we probably want the A road as it's the main road—and we've been on it since leaving the highway from London. The other road might be a *B* road, which are usually smaller and windier."

"I wonder what the Ramsgate Hill is," George said. "Sounds like it must be something major if a sign mentions a way to avoid it."

Nancy arched an eyebrow as she stared at George. "That doesn't sound like you, Fayne—to be scared of a hill."

George laughed. "I'm curious to see it, actually. Let's see which road goes by Moorsea Manor." After rummaging in the glove compartment, she took out a colorful brochure and quickly scanned it. "Well, the driveway to Moorsea Manor is definitely off the *A* road. We're supposed to turn right on it two miles after leaving Lower Tidwell. Obviously we should stay on the *A* road. But I wonder how much farther it is to Lower Tidwell? The brochure says it's about four hours from London."

Nancy glanced at her watch. "We've been on the road four hours. It's one o'clock now. We should be getting there any second."

"Hooray!" George said, in a tone of relief. "So what are we waiting for? The *A* road it is."

Nancy pressed the accelerator of the small silver-colored sedan, guiding it onto the right-hand fork. After she took the turn, the road suddenly narrowed. "Weird," she commented, eyeing the high privet hedge that was now inches from her window. "If this is the main road, I'd hate to see what the other road is like."

"We'd have been squished, for sure," George said. Twigs from the hedge scraped against her half-opened window, shedding tiny leaves into her lap as the car went by.

The road veered sharply left. Nancy swung the steering wheel hard. With its wheels squealing, the car followed the curve.

Nancy's eyes widened in disbelief. Before she had a chance to realize what was happening, she was heading up the steepest hill she'd ever driven on. The car appeared to shoot straight into the air, at what seemed to be a ninety-degree angle, although Nancy realized that would be impossible. Are we going to flip over backward? she wondered.

The car skidded. Nancy caught her breath, her thoughts racing. If these wheels can't get traction, she realized, the car will slip backward—all the way down the long, steep hill.

2

An Angry Exchange

The car clung to the road. The smell of burning rubber from the whirring tires stung Nancy's nostrils.

"Come on!" Nancy said, willing the car to go forward. She gritted her teeth and pressed the accelerator as far as it would go. For one sickening moment the engine let out a high-pitched whine, as if it was about to give out. Nancy glanced over at George, her heart in her mouth.

George stared wordlessly at Nancy, her face sheet white.

Once more, Nancy gunned the motor. The car lurched forward. Then, like a rocket bursting into space, it shot up the hill. With its wheels screaming for traction, it hurtled to the top, where the road immediately flattened out and the privet hedge abruptly stopped.

Nancy blinked in amazement. They were on a promontory overlooking the sea, with views of the water for miles. Closer to them, flocks of birds dipped over the hillsides, their swift dark shadows racing over the purple gray heath.

Nancy pulled the sedan to the side of the road. Taking a deep breath, she hunched over the steering wheel to steady her racing nerves. Then she stole a glance at George.

George was looking at Nancy as if she'd seen a ghost. "If that sign told us to go this way to avoid the other hill," George said, "I'd hate to think what that other hill is like!" She cast a glance back over her shoulder.

"There couldn't be a worse hill in the whole of England than the one we just went up!" Nancy exclaimed. She paused, then added thoughtfully, "I wonder if that sign was meant for the other fork."

George furrowed her brow. "Meant for the other fork?" she echoed. "But the sign was definitely on the right."

"But remember the hole in the ground on the left?" Nancy asked. "I wonder if the sign really belonged there but somehow got switched."

"Switched?" George said, considering. "That hill we went up was a monster, all right. I'll bet it was the hill the sign meant."

11

"Uh-huh. I just wonder whether the sign was switched on purpose."

"I don't know, Nan," George said doubtfully. "I know you love to solve mysteries, but there's probably a simpler explanation here. Maybe a road-construction crew took the sign down while working and then replaced it at the wrong fork by mistake. Simple enough, huh?"

Nancy frowned. "I don't think road-construction crews are that clueless, George. Their companies could be sued big time if some-one got hurt because they were careless. Plus, there was a hole where the sign was meant to go, and a road crew would have seen that. I'll bet that sign was switched on purpose—maybe by some kid on a dare."

"We'll probably never know," George said.

Nancy shrugged. "We should at least tell the police about the sign once we get to Moorsea." She pulled up the sleeve of her lavender shirt and checked her watch. "I'm really anxious to get there. It's past lunchtime already, and I could use one of those soothing cups of tea the English are so good at making."

"Or maybe a quick jog by the sea to take the tension away," George said, as Nancy pulled the sedan back onto the narrow road. "One thing's for sure," she added. "If that hill was the price we had to pay to get this awesome view, then maybe it was worth paying."

Nancy chuckled. "Maybe."

Five minutes later the girls reached a cluster of ancient stone houses with thatched roofs. Far below, the English Channel sparkled a bright blue green. The briny smell of the sea filled the air as Nancy drove down narrow lanes bordered by rose-covered stone walls.

"This must be the outskirts of Lower Tidwell," Nancy remarked. As she spoke, they passed a post office, a pub called the Wily Fox, a bookstore, a grocer's, and a single modern building.

"Outskirts—no way," George countered. "This *is* Lower Tidwell. Or should I say was?"

Through her rearview mirror, Nancy could see the village quickly receding. She smiled. "Then let's get back on the A road. We just have another two miles to go."

A few minutes later a paved driveway appeared on their right. Nancy slowed and turned into the open wrought-iron gates. Carved into the walls on both sides of the drive were the words Moorsea Manor.

"Well, it's about time," George said.

Nancy smiled to herself. Despite George's wry tone, Nancy noticed that her friend was sitting forward in her seat, her brown eyes sparkling with eager curiosity.

"Look, Nan," George said excitedly, as if reading Nancy's thoughts. "The grounds are like

13

something out of a movie. They're so grand—and we haven't even seen the house yet."

The long driveway curved through a parklike area of majestic old trees scattered over wide lawns. Meadows dotted with sheep opened on the right. Soon, two large stone buildings appeared. Behind them, another field filled with sheep rose into a wooded hill.

"Those must be the barns," Nancy commented. "The big one is probably for the sheep. I'll bet the small one's for the horses."

Next to the barns were a complex of greenhouses, vegetable gardens, and a couple of small stone buildings with signs saying Bakery and Wool Gathering.

"Didn't the brochure say that the estate sells its own bread and cakes to the public?" George asked. "And also woolen handknits like sweaters and scarves? Well, those must be the shops."

"This place is like some sort of feudal village," Nancy commented. "It has everything. Now all we need is the manor house." Just as she spoke, a tennis court came into view. On the other side of it was a stone wall with a high arched entrance through which Nancy caught glimpses of brightly colored flowers—the garden, she guessed.

George brightened at the sight of the tennis court. "I've seen everything except a baseball diamond," she remarked.

"Baseball's way too American for Moorsea

Manor," Nancy said. "But I wouldn't rule out cricket."

Several moments later a large stone house rose up behind a row of tall pine trees. With its splashes of ivy around windows and balconies, it seemed to be full of history, as if it had sheltered many families throughout the centuries and planned to give shelter to many more. Climbing roses crept up beside all the lower windows. The tiny leaded panes of the old windows sparkled in the afternoon sun as the girls drove closer.

"Wow," George said. "It's beautiful. And even though it's big, it looks like it could be cozy on a long winter evening."

Nancy grinned as the soft late-summer breeze blew through the car. "Well, I'm glad we won't have to test that theory on this vacation."

Nancy pulled the car up in front of the house. A short flight of marble steps led up to a large oak door with an elegant fan window above it. She turned off the ignition, relieved that the long trip was finally over.

Just then the oak door burst open. A tall, gray-haired man in his sixties wearing a perfectly pressed suit stormed out of the house. His pale blue eyes were slits of fury as he stared into the distance. His lips were drawn together in a tight angry line.

Before Nancy and George could move, a pretty young woman with long red hair followed him out the door. Dressed in white slacks and a hot pink sleeveless blouse, she tilted her face toward him with a puzzled, anxious frown.

The man whirled around, facing her. "A likely story, Mrs. Peterson!" the man fumed. "I've never been so insulted in my life. I'm leaving this hovel, and the sooner the better!"

3

A Shadow at the Window

Nancy and George exchanged glances.

"Nancy!" the man shouted in a bossy tone. "Come here this instant!"

Nancy started, shooting a puzzled gaze toward him. Before she had a chance to make sense of the situation, a stout older woman bustled out of the house, followed by a young, dark-haired man carrying two suitcases.

"Ah, there you are, Nancy, dear," the man said, patting the woman on the back of her starched white blouse as if she were a child. "Let's not linger. The fewer words we exchange with these wretched people, the better."

"But, darling, I want to make sure I've got

everything," the woman said. Her hands fluttered around her head in an agitated gesture. "My hat! I must have left it upstairs."

At that moment a large English sheepdog bounded out of the house. Clenched in its jaws was a large straw sun hat trimmed with fake flowers.

"Maisie!" the red-haired woman said in a horrified tone. "Drop it!"

The dog eyed the woman from under its mop of hair. Then it shook its head hard, wrestling the hat to the ground and ignoring the order.

"My brand-new hat!" the older woman exclaimed, wringing her hands. "Put it down, you miserable creature!"

In one deft move, the red-haired woman pried the hat from the dog's jaws and handed it to the older woman. "I'm so sorry—" she began.

"Hmmph! I can assure you that that's the least of the insults we've endured," the man spat out. His wife stared in distress at the shredded brim of her hat as if she wasn't so sure.

"Come along, Nancy dear," the man went on, "and you, too, Peterson. You can take our belongings to the car." He cast a withering glance over his shoulder at the dark-haired man who was hefting the suitcases down the front stairs.

"There's simply nothing more we need to discuss here."

The older man and his wife descended the stairs and headed toward a small parking area at the side of the house. The younger man rolled his eyes at the red-haired woman before trudging along obligingly behind the older couple.

"Whew," George muttered. "Well, here we are."

"I wonder why that man's so mad," Nancy said, unstrapping her seat belt.

George shrugged. "I don't know, but I sure am glad he's leaving."

Nancy opened her door and stepped outside into the soft afternoon air. The smell of roses wafted gently on the breeze.

Nancy and George walked toward the red-haired woman. Preoccupied, the woman held the dog's collar, frowning into the distance.

"Settle down, Maisie," she whispered as the dog whined and strained to follow the others. "Don't fret. Those nasty people will leave in a minute, and we won't have to see them ever again."

Nancy cleared her throat, and the woman raised her head abruptly. Without any warning, the dog jumped toward Nancy, paws outstretched. Like a dancing bear, it waddled upright on its hind legs for a moment, panting eagerly.

"Maisie!" the woman cried, clinging desperately to the dog's collar. "Down!"

"That's okay," Nancy said. As soon as the dog sat, Nancy reached down to pat her. "I love dogs."

"So do I," George echoed. "And what a cutie. Her name is Maisie?"

The woman nodded. "Yes, this is Maisie—she's only ten months old, but almost full grown and bursting with energy, as you can see." Then, as if taking in the girls for the first time, the woman squared her shoulders, smiled, and extended her hand. "And I'm Annabel Peterson. You must be Nancy Drew and George Fayne."

After shaking hands with the girls, Annabel went on, "I'm so sorry you had to witness that little scene. We must have seemed horribly rude not rushing to welcome you the moment you arrived. What an awful introduction to Moorsea Manor." She gave them a charming smile. "Usually, Hugh and I manage a bit better than that."

Judging by the tiny lines across her forehead, Nancy guessed that Annabel was about thirty. A simple black band secured her long red hair, which swept elegantly down her back, and her large hazel eyes shone out at the girls from under thick lashes. A dusting of freckles covered her ski-jump nose, giving her a youthful air.

Nancy smiled. "You don't have to apologize. That man would make anyone feel uneasy. I thought he seemed kind of—" She paused, searching for the perfect word to describe the man's unsettling anger.

"Wacko," George cut in. "Pardon me for being so blunt, but that guy was really off his rocker. Who was he, anyway?"

"His name is Lord Calvert," Annabel replied. She shook her head as if trying to banish him from her mind, then forced a grin. "Here, let me help you with your bags," she offered cheerfully. "You girls must be positively exhausted."

Nancy suddenly wasn't tired. She was feeling too curious about Lord Calvert's strange behavior to let the subject drop.

"Oh, thanks," Nancy said, responding to Annabel. "But first, please tell us more about Lord Calvert, if you don't mind. Why was he so mad?"

Annabel drew in a deep breath. "Well, I hate to color your arrival at Moorsea by telling you an unpleasant story," she began. "But if you insist . . ." Her eyebrows drew together in a troubled frown as she went on. "As you no doubt noticed,

21

Lord Calvert is a rather pompous old man. He's a long-standing member of Parliament, and he never, *ever* lets you forget it." She paused, flashing the girls a wry half-smile. "At least, he didn't let me forget it during the very brief time he was here."

"He's a member of Parliament?" George asked.

"Yes, in the House of Lords," Annabel explained. "Parliamentary members vote on various issues affecting our country, similar to the way your Congress operates. There are a few differences, though. One big difference is that a lord inherits his seat in Parliament. In the United States, of course, senators and congressmen are elected, as are our members of the House of Commons."

"So Lord Calvert thinks he's a big shot?" George prompted.

"That's putting it mildly," Annabel replied. "He can do no wrong, while others can do no right."

"You say he was here only briefly?" Nancy asked. "What happened in such a short time to make him fly off the handle like that?"

At that moment Maisie, who had been sitting obediently beside Annabel, shot down the stairs, letting out a series of eager, high-pitched barks. Turning, Nancy saw the young, dark-haired man who had helped Lord and Lady Calvert with their bags. He leaned down, tousling the puppy's mop of white hair that hung over her sharp black eyes.

Joining Annabel, he said, "Hello, darling, That was a pleasant little incident, wasn't it?" He gave a wry chuckle, then fixed his blue-eyed gaze on Nancy and George.

Annabel immediately introduced them to her husband, Hugh Peterson.

"Take my advice," Hugh said to Nancy and George, "and pretend you had amnesia from the time you drove into Moorsea until this moment. That way, your first impression of the place will be a good one." He gave his wife a fond smile, then hopped down the stairs to the car and popped open the trunk. Within seconds he had disappeared into the house, carrying Nancy's and George's suitcases.

"Please go on with your story, Annabel," Nancy urged. "You were just about to tell us why Lord Calvert was so mad."

Annabel arched an eyebrow. "It was such a little thing—but also very odd. As I was saying, he and his wife had just arrived, planning to stay the weekend, and Hugh and I had just shown them up to their room. It's our nicest room— large and airy, with a fantastic view of the sea. Of course, we thought they'd love it. And they did, until"—she paused, and her expression clouded over—"until Lord Calvert looked at his bureau. He nearly had a heart attack."

"But . . . why?" Nancy asked.

Annabel shook her head, puzzled. "I don't know how it got there, but right on top of his bureau was a large framed photograph of Tobias Jacobs. He's Lord Calvert's longtime parliamentary rival."

"His rival?" George echoed.

Annabel nodded grimly. "Jacobs and Calvert have been feuding for years on almost every political issue. At this point, they hardly speak. Lord Calvert was convinced that Hugh and I had placed that photo on his bureau as a practical joke because we secretly share"—she paused for a moment, then said—"how did he put it? Because we secretly share 'the same ridiculous political ideas as that hothead Jacobs.'"

"He can't be serious," Nancy said. "Why would you want to play a joke on one of your guests?"

"Of course, we wouldn't," Annabel said. "But Lord Calvert was so mad he couldn't think straight. That photograph had the same effect on him as the color red has on a bull. He completely lost his temper."

"Whew. I'll say," Nancy agreed. "You'd think

Moorsea's great reputation would have counted for something with him."

Annabel shrugged. "Apparently not. But he's such an egomaniac, maybe it's just as well he's gone. Though I hate to sound unwelcoming toward my guests."

"Well, I won't be losing any sleep over the old coot," Hugh said flatly as he emerged from the house.

"Not when we've got more pressing worries," Annabel said. Then furrowing her brow, she mused, "For instance, since we didn't put the picture on his bureau, who did?"

Nancy thought for a moment. Was someone out to annoy Lord Calvert in particular? she wondered. Or was the person who put the photo on the bureau really trying to upset the Petersons? Turning to Annabel, she asked, "Have there been any other strange things happening around Moorsea Manor lately? Has any other guest complained about anything?"

Annabel and Hugh exchanged thoughtful glances. Annabel frowned, then looked back at Nancy. Just as she was about to answer the question, a dark-colored object shot down from above. Missing Nancy's head by an inch, it crashed onto the marble stairs.

Everyone jumped. The object skidded to a halt by Annabel.

There was a moment of stunned silence. Then Annabel bent down to pick it up. Wide-eyed, she turned it around in her hands. Nancy could see the object was a bronze horse, about six inches high. The sheen had worn off its surface, and several small dark splotches shone through. It's definitely an antique, Nancy thought.

"My paperweight," Annabel murmured, frowning in confusion. "My father brought it back from India when he was a young man. I keep it on my desk."

Nancy looked up at the second-story window directly above them. A dark shadow quickly retreated from view.

4

Treasure-Hunt Terror

Nancy sprang into action. With the others on her heels and Maisie barking, Nancy flung open the main door and ran into the house. A wide curving staircase with a polished dark-wood banister rose up from the marble foyer. In five quick bounds, Nancy reached the staircase and sprinted up to the second floor.

At the top of the stairs, a large bay window opened out from the upstairs hall. A cushioned window seat curved around the bay in a semicircle. The mullioned window, which opened out, was slightly ajar, and Nancy judged that it overlooked the front door. Nancy frowned, checking both ways down the corridor. Except for Annabel, Hugh, and George, there was no sign of anyone else.

Nancy strode over to the window seat and peered down at it. Her heart skipped a beat. Was there really a vague indentation in the cushion? she wondered. The impression of someone's knee? Reaching down, she ran her finger over the red velvet fabric. There was a definite dip in it, she concluded. Clearly, someone had just been kneeling here.

She met Annabel's troubled gaze. In a shaky voice, Annabel said, "Someone must have leaned out the window, seen us talking, and then dropped the horse on purpose."

"Darling," Hugh said soothingly. "You don't know that. Whoever was here could have been leaning out the window for some harmless reason and then dropped the horse by mistake."

Annabel shot him a withering glance. "But before the person so innocently dropped it, he— or she—went into our office downstairs and stole the horse from my desk. At the very least, the person is a thief, if not a premeditating murderer."

Hugh dropped his gaze. "Quite right," he agreed.

A clock chimed from downstairs, and Nancy stole a look at her watch. It was the middle of the afternoon. A hush filled the house. No one besides the four of them was in sight—not a houseguest, not a housemaid. A soft breeze lifted the gauze window curtains, and the leaded panes threw rainbow glints on the polished oak floor.

"Is it all right if I look around?" Nancy asked, scanning the hall.

"Yes, but let me knock on all the closed doors," Annabel suggested, "since the guests know me. Also I have the master key. Let's also look in the linen closet." Nancy and George watched as she opened a nearby door. Shelves of neatly folded sheets and towels lined the walls. Otherwise, the closet was empty. While Annabel and Hugh hurried to check out the rooms, Nancy studied the upstairs hall.

A plush Oriental runner in bold colors of maroon, mustard, and navy stretched the length of it. She took a couple of running steps on it, listening for sounds.

"That carpet would have muffled anybody's footsteps," George observed, echoing Nancy's thoughts.

Nancy grinned. In a low voice, she said, "You've been with me on so many cases, Fayne, you can tell exactly what I'm thinking."

George cupped her hand behind her ear and leaned toward Nancy. "Case?" she said in a mocking tone. "Did I hear the word *case?*"

Nancy smiled as she pushed George away. "Shh! I'm trying to think." Once more, her eyes roamed the hall. Every few yards, the cream-colored walls were broken by mahogany doors—all closed except the one at the far end of the hall.

Nancy trotted down the hall and poked her head into the room. It was huge, with a king-size canopied bed in the center covered with a light-blue satin spread. Through the windows, the turquoise-colored sea lay spread out like a bright cloth at the end of the wide green lawn.

Nancy's eyes darted to the bureau beside the bed. A gleaming silver picture frame reflected the afternoon sun in a blaze of light. Inside the frame, a pudgy-faced man with curly salt and pepper hair grinned out impishly. He must be Tobias Jacobs—Lord Calvert's rival, Nancy mused.

After checking the closet and bathroom in Lord Calvert's room, Nancy joined the Petersons and George, who were talking together by the bay window.

Annabel forced a smile as Nancy approached them. "The bedrooms were empty—not a soul inside," she said. "I was just telling George that I'm so sorry your arrival has been troubled by these peculiar incidents. First Lord Calvert storming off and now the dropped horse." She gave an exasperated shrug. "I can't imagine why these things are happening."

Nancy bit her lip, suddenly remembering the road sign. "I doubt this has anything to do with the tricks at the inn," she began, "but I think the police should be told about it."

After Nancy described the road-sign incident, Annable promised to alert the police the moment she returned to her office downstairs. "Sounds a bit dangerous for motorists," Annabel commented. "I'm sure they'll want to switch that sign back right away."

"Have any other strange incidents happened around here?" Nancy asked.

Annabel's hazel eyes grew dark as she slumped down on the window seat. "Actually, yes," she began. "Yesterday evening, one of our guests ordered the inn's Wednesday dinner special, lamb marinated in plum sauce. Somehow, he received tough meat loaf with a dollop of whipped cream on it instead! Neither Hugh, nor I, nor any of the kitchen staff could imagine how that happened."

"Weird!" George exclaimed. "It's like some sort of practical joke."

"Yes," Hugh said darkly. "And a really bad one at that. You see the guest, Nigel Neathersfield, happens to be a quite well-known restaurant critic. A good report from him about our food would mean a lot of wonderful publicity for us. Needless to say, a bad report could sour our hard-earned popularity overnight."

"It seems so unfair that one person's opinion could undo all your hard work," George said.

"Well, that's the way this business is," Annabel remarked with a resigned shrug. "Cutthroat. Nice inns and restaurants like ours depend on word of mouth, which can be very fickle. One not-so-great meal or one bad hotel experience can really change a place's luck. We may be the trendy hotel to stay in right now, but who knows what might happen next month?"

"It sounds as if this person knows personal details about your guests," Nancy pointed out. "Lord Calvert's history with Tobias Jacobs, for instance—and I'm sure Nigel Neathersfield was chosen for the dinner joke because he's a restaurant critic."

The Petersons nodded in agreement. "Fortunately, Nigel didn't storm off the way Lord Calvert did," Annabel said. "He accepted our apologies and believed us when we told him we were in the dark about what had happened. Still, he wasn't happy."

"Who was the last person to see his plate after the lamb was put on it?" Nancy asked.

"Me," Annabel answered. "I do most of the cooking, with two assistants, Peggy and Faith. With Nigel's dish, I remember arranging the lamb, vegetables, and garnish on his plate and then putting it on the counter for the waitress to pick up and serve."

"Didn't she notice that the dish looked kind

of . . . odd?" George asked. "I mean, whipped cream on meat loaf? Come on."

"She was new—helping out just for the evening," Annabel explained. "She wasn't too aware of things. Usually, Hugh waits on our guests, but last night he was attending to the birth of some lambs. Someone must have switched the meal on the pantry counter when everyone in the kitchen was too busy to notice."

"A fast piece of work, too," Hugh grumbled. "We don't leave plates unattended for more than a minute at the most. We like to serve them piping hot." He shot Nancy an uneasy look. "Who could be playing these tricks on our guests?"

Nancy pursed her lips, thinking. The person might be another guest, she reasoned, or else someone who was lurking around Moorsea Manor. The trouble was, she mused, these incidents weren't just silly, harmless tricks. That dropped horse was no joke.

"Mmm, what's that delicious smell?" George asked. She sat up in bed, stretching after her nap. Sunlight slanted through the windows onto the chintz curtains and matching bedspreads. The ceiling of their room was low and crossed by dark wooden beams. Even so, it felt spacious and airy.

Nancy yawned from the canopied twin bed

next to George's, then immediately looked at her watch. "Wow! It's already eight, George. The sun sets later here because we're so far north. I bet we're missing dinner." Throwing off the covers, she jumped out of bed, then quickly began digging through her suitcase.

"The jet lag made us do it," George quipped. "Let's hurry down before all the food's gone."

The girls quickly dressed, then headed downstairs for dinner. But as they reached the foyer, guests were already streaming out of the dining room.

"Nancy, George," Hugh said, rushing up. "We saved you some supper. It's being kept warm in the kitchen."

"How about a game of backgammon later?" a childish voice asked. Glancing to her right, Nancy saw a blond-haired girl of about twelve gazing at her earnestly.

Nancy gave her a thumbs-up. "And my friend, George, will play the winner," she promised.

After eating roasted chicken and a fresh garden salad, Nancy and George joined the other guests in the living room. A fire roared in a cavernous stone fireplace while guests lounged around the room in armchairs or sofas—talking, reading, or playing board games. A stout man with mahogany-brown hair and a nose like a hawk's beak jumped up from his chair. "Hullo, girls," he said, extending his hand. "I'm Desmond Macmillan-Brown, and this is my wife, Lucy."

An athletic-looking woman with bright pink cheeks stood up and shook hands with the girls. "And this is our daughter, Ashley," she added in a loud, hearty voice, beckoning to the blond girl who was setting up the backgammon board.

Nancy smiled. "I'm Nancy Drew, and this is my friend, George Fayne," she explained.

"And please meet Georgina Trevor and Nigel Neathersfield," Mr. Macmillan-Brown added.

Georgina, who Nancy judged was in her early forties, looked up from her book with a tremulous smile. Running a hand distractedly through her graying auburn hair, she quickly dropped her gaze without saying a word. But Nigel Neathersfield, the restaurant critic, shot forward from his jigsaw puzzle to meet the girls.

"Well, you have the whole cast of characters here tonight, except Malcolm," he said, sweeping the room with his arm.

"Malcolm?" George echoed.

"Aye, Malcolm Bruce, the handsome Scot," Nigel said, imitating a Scottish brogue. "He's probably off partying at the Wily Fox, the hot spot in Lower Tidwell. He just arrived today, but even one evening here would probably be too dull for him."

Nancy perked up, curious to learn more about Malcolm, when Ashley announced the beginning of the backgammon game. Oh well, Nancy mused as she took a seat opposite Ashley, George and I are sure to meet Malcolm sooner or later.

No sooner had she sat down when a cute sandy-haired guy about her age strode into the room. Ashley jumped up eagerly and ran over to him, then tugged on his sleeve to bring him to meet Nancy and George. "It's so exciting to have Malcolm here," Ashley gushed after introducing him to the girls. "In case you don't know, Malcolm is a star on tellie, a show called *In My Face* here in England. Mum and Dad sometimes let me watch it."

"Ashley, you flatter me too much," Malcolm said with a charming grin. Then he turned toward George and said in a low voice, "I'm glad to see that things are finally livening up around Moorsea. Can I interest you in some backgammon, George? Then the winners of each game can play."

"Cool—a tournament," George said happily. "Okay, sure, let's get started."

The next morning at breakfast George leaned toward Nancy and murmured, "At least there were no more weird incidents at the inn last night."

Before Nancy could respond, Ashley Macmillan-Brown skipped over to their table.

"It's Friday—hooray!" Ashley said, clapping

her hands. "I've been looking forward to it all week."

Nancy smiled at the slender girl with dancing gray eyes. "What's so special about Friday?" she asked.

"You'll see," Ashley teased. She darted back to her parents' table.

Nancy and George traded glances. But no sooner had they finished a delicious breakfast of scrambled eggs, bacon, and hot cross buns than Annabel strode into the room.

Standing in front of the huge marble fireplace, Annabel said, "Good morning! I hope all of you will join me for my weekly treasure hunt. It's my favorite special event here at Moorsea Manor, and I hope you'll like it, too. Anyone who's interested, please assemble in the front hall at ten o'clock."

Ashley ran back to Nancy and George. "It's Mrs. Peterson's most popular event," she told them confidentially. "I can't wait." Ashley leaned over their table and scooped up the last remaining hot cross bun. She asked George if she could have it.

George nodded and Ashley took off again. "A treasure hunt?" George asked Nancy. "I wonder what it's all about."

"I read about it in the inn's brochure," Nancy said. "Apparently, Moorsea Manor has a bunch of special events, like a round-robin tennis tournament, a croquet competition, and on Fridays this treasure hunt. I'd forgotten all about it till now."

"So what's the treasure?" George wondered.

"Not money, definitely, but something like a gift certificate at Wool Gathering or a basket of homemade jams," Nancy explained. "After all, the hunt's mainly for fun, so I doubt the Petersons would want their guests to get too cutthroat about winning."

"I remember treasure hunts at birthday parties when we were kids," George mused. "They were a blast."

Nancy smiled. "I'm sure this one will be more challenging, since it's designed for grown-ups. Annabel makes up six clues for each person, except the sixth clue is the same for everyone. The first person to find the sixth clue wins."

"May the best guest win," George said, raising her glass of orange juice in a toast.

At ten o'clock, Nancy and George filed into the downstairs foyer along with the other guests. Maisie hopped around on her big soft feet, angling for attention.

Standing by the front door, Annabel quickly explained the rules. Then she added, "About three-quarters of a mile north of the house is a peat bog. It's extremely dangerous, so please don't venture off any obvious paths. All the clues for the hunt will be hidden within a half-mile distance of the house." She flashed the group a reassuring smile. "Good luck to all. And I hope everyone has a wonderful time—that's the main thing."

Annabel distributed a small folded paper to each guest. The guest's first name along with the number one was written neatly in black marker on the outside of the paper.

Nancy and George wandered outside, opening their papers.

"Hmm," Nancy said. "Clue Number One. 'Proceed to the feed bucket in the black lamb's stall.'" She shot a look toward the sheep barn. "Well, I guess I'm headed thataway." She pointed toward the large stone building several hundred yards to the right of the house.

"And I'm off to the sundial in the rose garden," George added as she studied her clue.

The two girls wished each other luck, then headed their separate ways. Nancy jogged toward the barn. Inside, the air smelled sweetly of hay. Stalls were lined up across from one another, with a wide center aisle. Nancy judged there were about thirty stalls in all.

How am I ever going to find the black lamb's stall? she wondered. Most of the stalls were empty—probably because during the day the sheep were outside grazing, she thought.

At the far end of the barn, Nancy stopped, her heart filled with delight. In the last stall five or six lambs frolicked, eagerly throwing themselves at one another, their ungainly legs splaying out around them.

Nancy glanced into the stall across the aisle. Inside, a tiny black lamb slept, curled up against its mother's belly. She unlatched the gate and slipped inside. Peering into the feed bucket, she drew out another folded piece of paper with the number two written on the outside.

" 'Hurry to the hollow of the oak tree beyond the beehives,' " she read.

Nancy stuck the clue in the pocket of her blue jeans skirt and ran out the backdoor of the barn. Nearby, she spotted a picket fence. Inside were some large white boxy structures. Beehives, she realized, catching sight of a warning sign nailed to the gate.

About twenty feet beyond the enclosure was a huge oak tree. Skirting the picket fence, Nancy rushed over to the tree and stuck her hand inside a large hole in the trunk at about eye level.

" 'Have a look at the mane of the brown- and white-spotted pony in the far pasture,' " she read after opening up the clue.

Several minutes later Nancy climbed a stile and went into a pasture she hoped was the far one. Nestled against a patch of woods, it seemed almost a half mile from the house.

Three ponies and two horses grazed there peacefully. Clipped to the mane of the brown-and-white pony was a piece of paper. Before

Nancy could remove it, a loud scream erupted from the nearby woods. "Help!" a voice cried. It was George!

Nancy sprinted over the pasture fence toward the scream. Once in the woods, she came to an open marshy area. To her complete horror, George was in the marsh sinking into the ground—it was already above her knees.

George was struggling to remove her legs, her arms flailing. Each time she tried to take a step, she sank farther into the black squelchy water of the bog. In a minute she'd be in over her head!

5

The Clue in the Quicksand

"Nancy, help me!" George shouted, her face showing her panic. She leaned toward Nancy, falling forward in the bog.

"Hang on," Nancy urged as George floundered in the soupy water. "I'll get you out."

Nancy cast a quick look around her and spied a long, sturdy-looking stick in the underbrush to her left. After making sure that the ground she stepped on was firm, Nancy retrieved the stick. Then she used it to poke the earth in front of her as she made her way carefully toward George.

The ground in front of her looked hard, with a greenish brown mossy surface. It might have been a forest path, but Nancy quickly realized the moss was just a thin cover hiding a treacherous bog. She could see how George had been fooled.

It's no use, she thought with dismay, testing the ground with her stick. It plunged through the moss into murky impenetrable swamp all around George, bringing up weedy tendrils of vegetation and black muck. There was no way Nancy could get close enough to help. By now, George had sunk in up to her hips.

"Hey, Nan, I'm going in fast," George said in despair. Nancy's heart thudded in her chest—George sounded so unlike her usual confident self.

A wide, flat stump a couple of feet away from George caught Nancy's eye. That just might work, she thought hopefully.

Nancy didn't waste a moment considering the danger she might face. Taking a deep breath, she made a flying leap onto the stump, holding tightly to her stick.

To her relief, the stump held firm as she landed on its flat center. Putting down her stick, she commanded, "Here, George, take my hands!" Then she leaned over and extended both arms toward George.

George grabbed on. Nancy pulled hard, trying to keep a grip on George's wet, slippery hands. But after a minute of straining to lift her out, Nancy realized she didn't have the strength to haul George from the bog.

"I'm going to try something else," Nancy announced, getting down on her knees. Careful not to lose her balance, she leaned forward, gripping George under both arms.

Nancy gave a ferocious yank. Bubbles erupted from the water as George moved forward an inch.

"It's working," Nancy grunted. "Come on, George. Try to help me. Pitch toward me. You can do it." She gritted her teeth and hauled, trying to ignore the pounds of muck that seemed determined to trap George forever in their depths.

A loud sucking sound and a horrible stench of rotting vegetation filled the air. Nancy, her arms around George, almost collapsed backward with relief. George was finally free!

"Ugh!" George groaned, clambering up next to Nancy on the stump. Her blue jeans were covered in slick black mud, and her hands were trembling uncontrollably. Otherwise, she seemed unfazed by her ordeal and grinned at Nancy gamely.

"Well, Nan," George said in a voice that was hoarse from shouting for help. "What do you say we get out of this joint? I'm not sure a basket of homemade jams is worth all this hassle."

Nancy shot George a lopsided smile. "That's the understatement of the year." Then her blue eyes studied George's mud-streaked face with

44

concern. "But seriously, are you all right? That was a deadly patch of quicksand."

George shuddered. "I had no way of knowing I was about to step into that stuff. At first, the ground under me was just a little wet and springy. Then suddenly, I plunged right through. No matter how hard I tried, I couldn't get out—it was as if invisible hands were dragging me down."

Nancy's gaze swept the bog. A number of dead trees were sticking up from the blanket of moss, like an army of thin gray ghosts. She shivered—she couldn't stand another second in this place. "Let's get out of here," Nancy said, tugging on George's T-shirt sleeve.

Carefully the two girls stood up. Nancy picked up her stick. Once more, she used it to find solid ground.

"So tell me, George," Nancy began, once the two were standing safely at the edge of the pasture. "How'd you get into that mess, anyway?"

George dug a clue out of her jeans pocket. "My fourth clue sent me to that stump in the bog. Before I saw that there was no clue there, the ground just swallowed me up. It was a totally weird feeling—I had no idea I was anywhere near the bog. I mean, it didn't occur to me that Annabel would write a clue that would send me into danger."

Nancy frowned as George handed her a piece of paper with the number four written in black marker on the outside. Sure enough, on the inside, in neat black print, the clue instructed George to proceed to the "first wide stump in the woods beyond the horse pasture, in front of the group of dead trees."

Nancy compared the writing with one of her clues. It looked the same, she thought, but the block print would be easy to imitate. She shot George a level look. "George, Annabel never would have made up a clue that sent you into that bog."

George's brown eyes searched Nancy's face. "Are you hinting that this is another trick someone's playing on the guests at Moorsea?"

Nancy nodded grimly. "Someone must have switched Annabel's clue with this one, which deliberately led you into danger." She pushed the clue back into George's fist. "These tricks may have started off being silly, but they're getting dangerous now."

"Yeah, that paperweight horse barely missed your head yesterday," George pointed out. "You could have been really hurt."

"Let's get back to the house right away," Nancy pressed. "We've got to tell Annabel what happened. Other people could have gotten bum clues, too."

As Nancy and George made their way back to

the house, Nancy felt a prickle of dread at the thought of what other guests might have encountered on the treasure hunt.

Near the sheep barn, Nancy saw a swift movement out of the corner of her eye.

"Isn't that Ashley?" George asked, pointing toward the beehive enclosure.

Just as George spoke, Ashley Macmillan-Brown slipped through a gate in the picket fence.

"Ashley, get out of there!" Nancy yelled. Didn't she see the warning on the gate? If Ashley got too near the bees, they might want to protect their hives and attack her.

Nancy ran toward Ashley, hoping the young girl would hear her warning.

A loud scream erupted from inside the fence. "Ashley!" Nancy shouted again.

Ashley screamed again. Then she tore back through the picket gate and moved toward Nancy and George.

A long dark line of bees shot out from the nearest hive. Swarming into an angry cloud, the bees headed straight for Ashley.

6

Manor House Mayhem

Ashley dove into Nancy's arms, cowering. The buzzing black cloud swooped up and away as Nancy hustled the girl into the barn.

"Are you okay, Ashley?" Nancy asked once they were safely inside.

"Did you get stung?" George asked, slipping through the door behind them.

"Ow," Ashley said, wincing as she rubbed her left leg. Tears brimmed in her eyes, but she immediately wiped them away. She looked away from the older girls in embarrassment. "I . . . I got a couple of stings on my leg when I first went in. I guess the bees were just trying to warn me away."

Nancy could tell Ashley was trying her best to

be brave. "Did your clue send you near the beehives?" Nancy asked her gently.

Ashley nodded, looking puzzled. "I was having so much fun. Then my third clue sent me inside the picket fence. But Annabel knows there are beehives there. Why would she have done that?"

"She wouldn't have," George said flatly. "We think some other person made up clues to endanger the guests."

Nancy searched Ashley's shocked face. "Did you notice a Keep Out—Bees sign posted on the fence by any chance?" she asked.

Ashley shook her head. Nancy peered out of the barn door, scanning the sky for bees. Then she motioned to the others that it was safe to follow. Outside, she pointed toward the picket fence and said, "Earlier, I saw a Keep Out sign on the fence, but now it's gone."

Nancy examined Ashley's clue. Like George's, its block print looked exactly like the writing on the regular clues.

"We've got to get back to the house and tell Annabel about this," George said with a weary sigh.

"She's going to have a fit," Ashley predicted.

Back at the manor house, several frantic guests were pacing the front hall while the worried-looking Petersons were trying in vain to calm them.

Georgina Trevor wandered aimlessly in circles,

her hands fluttering around her heart. "I tell you," she muttered in a high childlike voice, "my nerves are simply shot."

Ashley dashed toward her mother. "Ashley, darling!" Mrs. Macmillan-Brown exclaimed, enveloping her daughter in a bear hug. "Daddy and I had the most awful fright. And Miss Trevor, too." She paused to stare at George. "My goodness! Look at you, George—all covered with mud."

Ashley tugged at her mother's sleeve, then pointed toward the red, swollen marks on her leg. Her mother caught her breath, looking at them aghast. "Ashley, what happened?"

First Ashley and then George quickly related their ordeals to a rapt audience. While Annabel hurried off to fetch a mixture of baking soda and water to soothe Ashley's bee stings, Hugh continued to console the guests.

Nancy turned to the elder Macmillan-Browns. "Please tell me—what was your awful fright?" she asked them curiously.

Mr. Macmillan-Brown fixed his round blue eyes on Nancy. "We were having a fine time on the hunt," he explained, "until one of our clues sent us into the stall belonging to the most ferocious ram at Moorsea. We barely escaped with our lives." He shot a scathing look at the Petersons. "It turns out that miserable heap of

50

wool has to be kept in isolation because of his ill temper. But were we told that earlier when it would have mattered? No!"

"Now, now, Desmond," his wife said, picking a piece of straw off a muddy spot on his polo shirt. "Annabel and Hugh are not to be blamed. They're as much in the dark as we are."

"Yes, but they didn't have to stare down a gigantic live sweater with the meanest temper in town!" he retorted.

"And I," Georgina Trevor broke in. She paused dramatically for a moment while everyone's attention shifted to her. "I slipped on a loose slate-roof shingle while trying to make my way to a drainpipe—following my clue's instructions, of course. I nearly slid off the roof to certain death on the stone driveway far below." She fished in the pocket of her dowdy-looking A-line skirt. "Now what did I do with that clue, anyhow? Oh, well—I can assure you it sent me astray."

"Miss Trevor," Annabel said, returning to the room with some salve for Ashley. "Once again, I'm so sorry that you almost fell. But I promise that neither Hugh nor I wrote up that clue. We would never have sent you onto the roof—it's almost vertical." She flicked back her long red hair with an air of helpless frustration.

"Well, someone did," Georgina said, peering stubbornly at the Petersons.

"That's right, *someone* did," a man's voice cut in. Everyone turned to look at Nigel Neathersfield, who had been pacing in grim silence in front of the marble fireplace.

"I was lucky," he went on, running a hand through his thick blond hair. "The Macmillan-Browns warned me off the hunt before I met with any trouble." His short, thin body gave an involuntary shiver as he scowled at the Petersons through tiny black eyes. "But I shudder to think what my fate might have been if I'd continued to follow my clues." He paused for a moment, then added portentously, "I wonder if that same person who so kindly provided me with a meat loaf dinner the other night is at work again."

"We have no way of knowing if it was the same person," Annabel protested. "Please, Mr. Neathersfield, try to believe that my husband and I are very upset by these tricks, too. We will do whatever we can to make things right around here again."

"Oh, I don't doubt you on that score," Nigel declared. "I'm sure you'd do anything for the sake of your business. Still, I feel it's my duty to report these events in my paper when I return to London on Sunday evening. The public has a right to be warned about what they might encounter here. In fact," he continued, gazing nonchalantly at Annabel's stricken face, "maybe

I should demand my money back now and clear out. I don't want to endanger myself—nor would I want to face another dinnertime disaster."

"Please, Mr. Neathersfield," Annabel begged, flashing Hugh a frantic look, "give us a chance. Stay calm, and we'll get to the bottom of this mystery straightaway."

"I expect no less," Nigel said tartly, turning on his heel and striding up the stairs.

"Annabel," Nancy said in a low voice, "may I talk to you privately?"

"Certainly," Annabel answered. After assuring her guests that she was available twenty-four hours if need be, she led Nancy into a room off the hall marked Reception.

The moment she sat, she dropped her face in her hands and burst into tears.

"Annabel!" Nancy said, rushing over and placing a comforting arm around her shoulders. "Don't cry! We'll figure things out."

"I'm sorry, Nancy," Annabel said, wiping her tears away. "This sort of behavior isn't like me at all. I'm normally quite professional—it's just that I'm strained to the breaking point. Someone is clearly out to strike a blow at Moorsea Manor. What if a guest gets hurt? And what if our business is ruined?" She cast a desperate look around the sunny room. "I'd lose this place."

Nancy sat down in a nearby chair. She'd been

53

looking forward to her vacation, but Annabel needed her help. Plus, she realized, that with a maniac loose at Moorsea, peace and quiet would be in short supply, even if she didn't agree to investigate.

Annabel shot her a curious look. "But why did you want to talk to me, Nancy?"

Nancy smiled. "To offer to help you find whoever is playing these tricks. You see," she added modestly, "I'm a detective."

Annabel's eyes shone. "You are? What a terrific stroke of luck! Well, if you'll take charge of this investigation, Hugh and I will do whatever we can to help you."

"Let's start with a few questions, then," Nancy said, sitting forward. "First, can you think of anyone who might bear a grudge against you?"

Annabel pursed her lips as she thought. "Yes, Billy Tremain," she answered after a moment. "He used to be the shepherd here, but we had to fire him two months ago for mishandling the birth of a pair of lambs. One of the lambs died because of Billy's carelessness. He was furious when we fired him. He has a very surly personality—so I wasn't sorry to see him go."

"Anyone else?" Nancy asked, filing Billy Tremain away in her mind as a possible suspect.

Annabel tapped a slender forefinger against her cheek. "I can't think of any other person who might bear us a grudge, but I can think of two people who would be absolutely thrilled if we went out of business."

"Really? Who?" Nancy asked.

"The Singh brothers. They're identical twins who are big developers in the area," Annabel explained. "They're hot to get their hands on Moorsea Manor so they can make a killing developing the land. If our inn fails, Hugh and I would have to sell Moorsea—and those Singh chaps would be first in the queue to buy it, I'm sure."

"Can you tell me what Billy and the Singh brothers look like and how I can track them down?" Nancy asked.

"Billy is short and stocky, with broad, strong-looking shoulders," Annabel told her. "He's got dark hair, green eyes, and a mole on his left cheek. I don't believe I've ever seen him smile. He lives in a ramshackle farmhouse about four miles away on the moor.

"As for the Singhs, they immigrated from India years ago and have an office on High Street in Lower Tidwell—they're realtors as well as developers. They're about thirty, tall and thin, dark haired and dark eyed, with hair-trigger tempers, I'm told. But I also hear they can be charming when it suits them."

"Is their business successful?" Nancy asked.

"Very," Annabel replied. "In fact, most people

think it's too successful. The countryside around here is so beautiful and unspoiled, and most people want it to remain that way. The Singhs have bought up land and subdivided it without regard to natural beauty or to the feelings of the community."

"I guess their business has made lots of money," Nancy remarked.

"Lots," Annabel said. "People around here are jealous of the Singhs' wealth. And they bitterly resent the fact that the money has been made at their expense—by tearing up the countryside that they all love."

Nancy nodded as she considered that information. "Thanks, Annabel," she said, standing up. "I'll start by investigating these guys, then. I'll see what clues I can turn up."

"Please be careful, Nancy," Annabel warned. "This person clearly means business—look what almost happened to George. And if he, or she, suspects you of spying—" She gave a small shudder.

"Don't worry. I'll be careful," Nancy assured her. "But please don't tell any of the other guests about my role. George and Hugh, of course, will be in on our secret—that's all."

Annabel extended her hand for Nancy to shake. "Nancy, I feel better already knowing you're on the case."

Nancy said goodbye to Annabel, then headed upstairs to tell George about the investigation. But George was not in their room. Steam coated the bathroom mirror, and George's muddy clothes lay in a heap on the floor. George had obviously just showered and changed, Nancy reasoned, but where could she have gone?

Nancy hurried outside, scanning the lawn and pastures from the front stairs. Could she be checking out the beach? Or maybe the sheep barn?

Nancy strode toward the barn. Inside, she heard a murmuring noise at the far end.

"George?" she began, walking toward the sound.

A young, dark-haired man jolted upright from where he'd been slouching over a stall door. He scowled angrily at Nancy, his dark eyebrows drawing together in a thick black line above green eyes. A large mole stood out prominently on his left cheek.

Nancy did a double take. This guy perfectly matched Annabel's description of Billy Tremain! But why was he lurking around here if he'd been fired? she wondered.

"Uh, do you work here at Moorsea?" she asked curiously.

"What's it to you, miss?" he asked, squaring a set of powerful-looking shoulders.

Nancy refused to lower her gaze. "I'm a guest here," she answered, "and I just wondered who you were."

Violently punching his left palm with his right hand, he began to stalk toward her. "Well, I'll thank you to keep your questions to yourself!" he growled in a menacing tone.

Nancy's heart raced. Was he actually going to attack her?

7

A Mysterious Sign

"Stop right there!" Nancy commanded, trying to take control of the situation. This guy looks as if he could tackle a bear, she thought. I'd better get ready to defend myself, just in case.

She glanced to her side, spying a small shovel a few feet away. But before she could make a move to grab it, Billy stopped, then quickly spun around. Without another word, he disappeared out the backdoor of the barn.

Nancy took a deep breath, then exhaled in relief. Annabel sure wasn't kidding when she described the guy's attitude, she thought grimly.

Nancy retraced her steps out of the barn, determined to find George. Maybe she's at the beach, Nancy thought. But just as she was heading across the lawn toward the sea, she caught sight of George jogging toward her, carrying two tennis racquets.

"Where have you been, Nancy?" George puffed as she reached her. "I've been hoping to scare up a game of tennis. These racquets belong to the inn, but I'm sure they'll do."

"I've been hunting for you, too, George," Nancy said. "Annabel—and I—think that someone may be playing these tricks to hurt the inn. She wants me to investigate; naturally, I need your help."

George grinned. "What did I tell you? You've already found yourself a mystery—and it's only our second day of vacation. Sure, I'll help out. Do you have any suspects yet?"

Nancy was about to answer when she noticed Malcolm Bruce, the Scottish actor, sneaking up behind George.

Malcolm's bright blue eyes twinkled as he touched his forefinger to his lips to silence Nancy. Then he clapped his hands over George's eyes.

George spun around. "Malcolm!"

"George!" Malcolm retorted, punching her playfully on the arm. "I see Nancy and you are aiming to get some shots in," he said in his Scottish brogue. Then he mimicked a tennis forehand stroke. "Well, may the best player win."

George laughed, then caught Nancy's expression. "Actually, Malcolm," George said firmly, "Nancy and I are busy now. I'm sure we'll be getting a game in later, though."

"Busy?" Malcolm asked. "Doing what?"

Making up a quick explanation, Nancy said, "George was just trying to get me to join her in a game but I've already told Ashley we'd play cards with her. We were just heading inside when you came along."

Nancy paused for a moment, chewing her lip in thought. She was hoping to track down Annabel to let her know about Billy, and she could certainly do that without George's help. "Well, I'm sure Ashley wouldn't mind if just I showed up," she added. "And I get the feeling George is really up for some tennis."

"Well, then, George," Malcolm said, flashing her a flirtatious grin, "I know I'm a poor substitute for Nancy. But if you don't mind my two left feet, I'd be honored if you would hit a few balls with me."

George's face lit up. "Two left feet, Malcolm— give me a break! I'm sure you'll cream me. Come on, let's nab that court before someone else does."

George and Malcolm headed toward the tennis

court while Nancy jogged to the house to search for Annabel.

Nancy found both Annabel and Hugh inside the reception office poring over correspondence. A look of alarm passed over Annabel's face as she took in Nancy's grave expression. Hugh closed the door and explained that Annabel had told him about Nancy's investigation. Then he and Annabel looked attentively at Nancy.

"I just saw Billy Tremain," Nancy declared, sitting down in a vacant chair. "At least, I think it was him." She told the Petersons the details of her confrontation in the barn.

"I'm sure that's who the chap was," Annabel said in distress. "Your description fits him to a *T.*"

Hugh pushed back his chair and jumped up, his blue eyes flashing angrily. "If I find Billy on our property, I'm going to make mincemeat of him."

"Be careful, darling, that he doesn't make mincemeat out of you," Annabel warned as Hugh strode furiously out of the room. Her voice fell to a helpless murmur as he rushed away, undeterred.

As soon as Hugh had gone, Nancy asked Annabel what she knew about the guests staying at Moorsea and the location of each guest's room.

"Do you really think a guest could be responsible for this mischief?" Annabel asked, surprised. "After all, guests are the ones who have suffered these awful tricks. Just think of the treasure hunt. Everyone faced danger except for Nigel, and he suffered ridicule at dinner the other night."

"Still, I don't want to rule anyone out yet," Nancy told her.

Annabel nodded thoughtfully. "Well, I don't know much more about our guests than you do, Nancy. They all seem on the up-and-up to me. I can't imagine why any of them would want to drive us out of business.

"As for the room setup, we've got six guest rooms on the second floor and a seventh on the third. Hugh and I live on the third floor, too, in a separate wing that has a private staircase leading up from the second floor."

Counting off on her fingers, Annabel went on, "The Macmillan-Browns are in Room One, Ashley is next to them in Room Two, you and George have Room Three, Nigel Neathersfield writes his annoying reviews in Room Four, Georgina Trevor hibernates in Room Five, and Room Six is empty this weekend because Lord and Lady Calvert left so suddenly. Malcolm Bruce stays on the third floor in Room Seven."

"Hmm, Malcolm Bruce," Nancy said, as a sudden realization crossed her mind. "You know, Annabel, I don't remember seeing Malcolm at the treasure hunt."

"That's right," Annabel said with a start. "He

63

wasn't there. He'd asked me not to make him any clues. He said he wanted to sleep late this morning."

"So he's the only guest who hasn't been the victim of a prank," Nancy went on. "Something bad has happened to every other guest." She looked at Annabel appraisingly, then asked, "Would you mind if I search his room? He's playing tennis with George now, so this would be the perfect time to check it out."

Annabel sighed. "He *is* our guest, though, Nancy," she said reluctantly. "I feel odd giving you a key to his room. I'm responsible for his privacy, after all. What if he catches you there?"

"Don't worry, I'll make up some excuse. And I definitely won't tell him you gave me permission to search his room," Nancy replied. "And what if he really is behind these pranks? We owe it to everyone here to check out that possibility."

Annabel's hazel eyes narrowed. "All right," she said, reaching for a key on a row of pegs labeled with room numbers. "I'll trust your judgment, Nancy. There are two staircases leading upstairs from the second floor—Malcolm's is the one directly across the hall from your room."

Nancy thanked Annabel as she took the key. Then she hurried upstairs to the third floor.

At the top of the stairs was a spacious foyer, lit by a large window, with a closed door facing her.

Nancy unlocked the door and stepped into a huge sunny room with windows on three sides. An unmade bed draped in red velvet took up most of the space on her left, several oil paintings of country scenes hung on the walls, and on her right a tall antique bureau reached almost to the ceiling. Against a nearby wall, an empty suitcase lay open on a luggage rack.

After shutting the door behind her, Nancy checked under the bed and on top of the night tables. Finding nothing, Nancy went to work on the bureau. She had to stand on a chair to see in the highest drawers, but after five minutes of careful searching among Malcolm's clothes, she'd turned up no clues.

Her gaze fell on a door next to the luggage rack. The closet, Nancy guessed. She placed the chair back against the wall and opened the door. Inside, three or four summer sports jackets hung neatly on hangers. Behind them, Nancy caught a glimpse of a white object propped in a corner, partly hidden by the coats. What in the world? Nancy thought. She pushed the jackets aside.

It was a white rectangular piece of wood nailed to a pole about her height. Black letters were painted on its surface.

Nancy's jaw dropped as the words jumped out at her: *B* Road, Scenic Drive, Danger—Extremely Steep Incline.

It's the road sign for the monster hill, Nancy realized. Malcolm must have stolen it—obviously as a prank. I'll bet he's guilty of the pranks at Moorsea, too, she reasoned.

A key rattled in the door. Nancy froze. Malcolm was back! But why so soon?

8

Missing!

Nancy leaped into the closet and shut the door. In the dark, she flattened herself into a corner. The sleeves of Malcolm's coats tickled her face. Her heart hammered against her chest.

She fixed her eyes in the direction of the door, hoping Malcolm wouldn't open it. To her frustration, there was no keyhole to look through—just a narrow space under the door through which a slender shaft of daylight shone.

Heavy footsteps thumped across the floor toward the closet. Nancy held her breath, expecting the door to be yanked open at any second.

A sudden loud vrooming sound tore through the air. Nancy jumped. A vacuum cleaner! She realized with relief that the maid must be there to clean Malcolm's room.

With her ear to the door, she listened to the maid's movements outside. After a while the vaccuum cleaner stopped, and Nancy heard the sound of running water on the other side of the closet wall. The maid must be in the bathroom, she reasoned—now is my chance!

She cracked open the door and cautiously peeked out. No one was there. Casting a look behind her, she caught sight of a woman in a neat blue dress vigorously mopping the bathroom floor.

Nancy's sneakers made no noise as she sprang across the bedroom and slipped through Malcolm's door. Seconds later she was at the bottom of the front stairs, pausing to catch her breath in the empty hall.

A man's hearty laugh blew in with the air from an open window. Then the front door flew open. George and Malcolm burst inside, their cheeks flushed from tennis.

"Nancy!" Malcolm said, his eyes sparkling. "Why didn't you warn me about your friend here? She belongs with the pros at Wimbledon— not trouncing innocent lads like me."

Nancy's thoughts shifted to the road sign in Malcolm's closet. Innocent? she wondered. Well, we'll see about that.

George smiled at Malcolm. "I'll bet you were

off your game today, Malcolm. If you hadn't double-faulted, I'd have been creamed for sure."

Malcolm's dimples deepened. "Shall we play again tomorrow, George? I'll have no self-respect if I don't try to save face."

"Done," George agreed, slapping Malcolm five. As Malcolm headed upstairs to change, Nancy tugged on George's arm and said, "It's already twelve-thirty, George. Do you want to drive into Lower Tidwell to get some lunch? I know they've got a buffet here on the front lawn, but I'd like to fill you in on some things I've discovered."

George nodded in understanding. "Sure thing, Nan. Just let me catch a quick shower."

Twenty minutes later Nancy and George were munching cucumber sandwiches and scones with clotted Devonshire cream and raspberry jam, and washing it all down with tea at the Marigold in the center of town. Lace curtains framed the windows of the cozy room, and vases of yellow marigolds decorated the tables.

Nancy placed a spoonful of clotted cream on a scone, then covered it with jam. "This is a real Devonshire specialty—clotted cream," she declared. "I know we should be eating a heartier meal at lunch, but I couldn't resist ordering a typical Devonshire tea. I mean, we might not have the chance later on today if the case heats up."

George grinned. "I'm just glad the waiter agreed to serve it to us now. Mmm—delicious," she added, eyeing Nancy's scone, "like having whipped cream on your scone instead of butter."

"That's why the English call this a 'cream tea.'"

After finishing her scone, Nancy filled George in on the details of the case so far. George frowned. "I don't know, Nancy," she said, putting down her cucumber sandwich to speak. "I don't blame you for being suspicious of Billy Tremain, but Malcolm? He's a really nice guy, and I think it's unfair to suspect him of these pranks. I mean, what could his motive be?"

"Maybe we just don't know his motive yet," Nancy pointed out. "But that sign in Malcolm's closet is proof enough for me that he likes to play practical jokes—even if we haven't found any clues that he did the stuff at Moorsea."

George frowned, and then shrugged it off. "Maybe the real person is trying to frame him," she remarked.

"Frame him?" Nancy said doubtfully. "By putting a road sign in a closet that no one would be likely to find? I don't know about that, George."

"Have you told Annabel and Hugh about the sign yet?" George asked.

"No. I don't want to stir things up, and they might want to call the police. The person might get scared away before we can find more proof."

The girls finished their meal in silence. On their way back to Moorsea Manor, Nancy said, "I'd like to spend the afternoon hunting for evidence in Billy Tremain's farmhouse. Are you game for a walk across the moors?"

George brightened. "Sure am," she replied.

As Nancy and George stepped out of their car at the inn, wisps of fog were curling up from the sea cliff at the edge of the lawn. "It looks like the afternoon might get foggy," Nancy commented.

"Let's check over that edge to see if the fog is coming in thick," George suggested. "Because if it is, we probably shouldn't go out on the moor. I've heard you can lose the path and step into a bog—there are a bunch of them around."

"And I'll bet that's not an experience you'd like to repeat," Nancy remarked dryly, smiling at George.

The girls jogged to the end of the lawn. At the bottom of the thirty-foot cliff was the beach. Wooden steps zigzagged down the rocky incline to the white sands below, where some rowboats

71

were pushed up on shore. A long dock jutted out into the sea.

Standing at the top of the cliff, Nancy could see a dark bank of fog rolling in. The pungent smell of moist salt air surrounded her. She shivered, rubbing her bare arms.

"Looks bad," George said.

Nancy nodded, chewing her lip. Maybe it would make sense for her and George to spend the afternoon at the inn questioning some of the staff. Someone might have noticed a person prowling around the inn—or some other detail that would provide the case with a much needed clue.

Nancy told George her thoughts. Then the girls separated, George to question the outdoor help—the shepherd and his helpers, the gardeners, and the shopkeepers at Wool Gathering and the Bakery—and Nancy to interview the household staff.

Promptly at six the guests at Moorsea Manor were assembled for drinks before dinner around a roaring fire in the living room. Mementos of the sea, from unusual shells and driftwood on the mantle to oil paintings of smugglers hiding their loot in seaside caves, decorated the room.

With a ginger ale in one hand and some cheese on a cracker in the other, Nancy shivered in her short peach-colored sundress. Stepping close to the fire, she said, "I didn't quite plan for these chilly English nights."

"Neither did I," George said, glancing down ruefully at her sleeveless red shift.

Nancy took a sip of her soda, then asked, "But tell me, how was your afternoon on the case?"

"Frustrating," George answered with a shrug. "No one I talked to noticed anything suspicious going on at the inn during the last few days."

"Same here," Nancy said, her eyes searching the room. The other guests seemed edgy. Some were chatting nervously in low tones; others were standing alone, fidgeting with drinks or hors d'oeuvres. They all looked as if they expected something horrible to happen at any minute.

Nigel Neathersfield strolled by, handing out menus. "Peggy, one of the cooks, just gave these to me to distribute," he explained to Nancy and George. He studied the menu. "I say, ladies, the chow looks great tonight— sheep's-milk cheese wrapped in grape leaves as an appetizer, organic baby greens from the kitchen garden for the salad, lamb chops with fresh mint from the herb garden, and chocolate soufflé with ginger-flavored whipped cream for dessert." He shot the girls a confidential look and added, "Though I'm half-expecting a bomb to explode in my soufflé." He chuckled wryly as he moved away.

Nancy peered at the menu, delighted at the delicious dinner it promised.

"Well, if it isn't my two favorite girls!" a flirtatious voice murmured over her shoulder.

Nancy wheeled around. Malcolm Bruce, wearing a jacket and tie, was smiling broadly at her and George, a glass of soda in his hand. "I feel much better," he went on with a sly wink at George, "now that I've had the afternoon to recover from our game. It's a shame the fog came in—I would have suggested a boat ride this afternoon."

"A boat ride? No, no, no!" said a tremulous voice at Nancy's elbow. Turning, she saw a demure Georgina Trevor in a ruffly knee-length dress patterned with pink and orange flowers. Georgina's reddish gray hair fell in wispy ringlets around her face as she shook her head gravely.

"Boats have been lost at sea in a fog like this one," Georgina went on. "You must never, never go outside in the fog—at sea or on land."

"I hear the moor can be treacherous in a fog on account of the quagmires," Malcolm remarked.

"Well, the quagmires—and the ghosts," Georgina pronounced.

"Excuse me?" George said.

Georgina dropped her gaze under the others' surprised stares. "Yes, the ghosts," she repeated nonchalantly. "Would you like me to tell you a ghost story about Dartmoor?"

Nancy glanced at the fog swirling outside the window. A line of fir trees screening the side of the house loomed through the mist like giant shadows laying seige. Otherwise, she could see nothing. "Dartmoor seems like a perfect setting for ghost stories," Nancy commented to Georgina.

"Maybe too perfect," Malcolm said with an anxious chuckle.

"Dartmoor abounds with ghost stories—and rightfully so because ghosts adore it," Georgina declared. "Moorsea Manor may not lie within Dartmoor, yet the atmosphere of the nearby moors reaches out to us. Let me tell you a true story. A friend of mine, when she was a little girl, lived in a nearby town. One foggy night she woke up, unable to sleep. She had a horrible feeling that all was not well. Suddenly a piteous whining sound filled the room. To her amazement, a lovely, sweet-looking terrier was sitting at the foot of her bed, whimpering as if its heart would break. She reached forward to cuddle it, but it disappeared the moment she touched it—"

"Pardon me," a man's voice broke in. Mr. Macmillan-Brown shuffled up between Nancy and George. "Has anyone seen either Peterson or his wife lately?" he asked. He reached inside his

75

vest pocket to check a pocket watch. "Usually they're here in the living room before six to greet guests and pour drinks. We've had to fend for ourselves getting drinks tonight, which is very annoying. Now it's almost time for dinner, and there's still no sign of them. Quite frankly, I'm getting hungry." He puffed up his chest and frowned.

Nancy felt a prickle of unease. Come to think of it, she hadn't seen the Petersons all afternoon—not since Hugh had stormed off to confront Billy Tremain. She hoped he and Annabel were both okay.

At that moment Hugh burst into the room, interrupting her thoughts. Glancing anxiously from guest to guest, he announced, "Sorry for the delay, ladies and gentlemen, but Annabel and I have a bit of a crisis on our hands. Our dog, Maisie, seems to be missing. Annabel and I have been frantic. But we plan to have dinner ready for you before too long." He paused, then added, "Needless to say, if any of you has seen Maisie this afternoon or evening, please let us know immediately."

Hugh disappeared into the front hall, and a shocked hush descended on the guests. After a few seconds everyone began to talk in low, nervous tones.

"The plot thickens," Mr. Macmillan-Brown

proclaimed in a voice of doom. Nancy didn't wait to hear any more. Without drawing attention to herself, she slipped out of the room.

Nancy crossed through the dining room and headed toward a swinging door that lead to the kitchen. The dining room table and a small side table were already set with white linen table-cloths, gleaming silverware, and crystal. A fire flickered gaily in the fireplace. A stag's head with antlers stuck out from the wall above the man-tle. Its startled-looking eyes surveyed the empty room.

Nancy's platform sandals clicked on the hard-wood floor as she entered a large butler's pantry, where Hugh was garnishing the first-course plates with sprigs of fresh parsley. His fingers trembled as he worked, and Nancy could tell he was very upset.

"I wanted to ask you more details about Maisie," she began. "When did you notice she was missing?"

"This afternoon. Annabel and I are beside ourselves. We love that dog." He shot her an anxious look. "I want to show you something, Nancy."

He slid open the door of a dumbwaiter nearby and handed Nancy a brown leather dog collar. "It's Maisie's," he explained. "I found it earlier on her dog bed in the kitchen, and I stashed it in the dumbwaiter for safekeeping. None of the kitchen help has the slightest idea who put it on her bed."

It wasn't the collar that caught Nancy's attention—it was the note attached to it by a piece of string, written in block letters. "Begone from Moorsea Manor," she read, "if you ever want to see your stupid mutt again."

9

Behind Closed Doors

Nancy examined the note, which was written on Moorsea Manor stationery. Begone? she mused. Give me a break. I mean, how many people in this century talk that way?

She met Hugh's anguished gaze. "I didn't tell the other guests this," he said, "but Annabel's upstairs in bed. She's too upset to oversee dinner tonight, so Peggy is handling the meal. Annabel wouldn't want anyone to think she's shirking her duties, though, so please don't tell the other guests."

"I won't," Nancy said. Her stomach churned as she thought of Maisie being kidnapped by someone. "Please, Hugh," she went on, "tell me everything you can remember about where and when you last saw Maisie. You noticed she was missing this afternoon?"

"Yes. Annabel last remembers seeing Maisie after the treasure hunt when everyone was gathered in the front hall describing their accidents. But she can't remember seeing her after you spoke with us about Billy Tremain being in the barn. Oh, and by the way, Nancy, I couldn't find Billy after I left you and Annabel so rudely." He flashed her an apologetic half-smile.

"I don't blame you for hurrying away to look for him," Nancy said. "Billy was trespassing. And if he is guilty of the pranks, that means he has Maisie with him now." Fingering Maisie's collar, Nancy asked, "Exactly when did you find this?"

"About five o'clock," Hugh answered. "Long after we first realized she was missing, which was shortly after I returned from scouting for Billy. It's very unusual that Maisie would be gone even for an hour—she's a real homebody, she doesn't roam."

Nancy cast her mind back over the events of the day. After interviewing the staff, she had taken a long walk on the beach and then headed upstairs to dress for dinner. She hadn't noticed anything suspicious at all.

"So you and Annabel called Maisie for a while?" she asked.

"Yes, we called her and looked everywhere we

could think of—the barn, the shops, the beach, everywhere. And then we found the note and collar." Hugh was almost pleading with Nancy. "What on earth is going on?"

"I don't know," Nancy said. "But I promise I'll get to the bottom of this. And I promise to find Maisie." Nancy stared down at the note. "Would it be okay if I keep this? I'd like to investigate it later."

At dinner Nancy and George invited Malcolm to join them. Unlike the merry atmosphere that had bubbled among the guests after dinner the previous evening, a gloom hung over the group. Each guest took a seat in silence. Mrs. Macmillan-Brown's forehead was creased with worry, and even the normally cheerful Ashley was glum. Georgina Trevor seemed even more distracted than usual, pouring water into her already filled glass and taking no notice of the puddle that quickly formed below it.

Everyone started as Nigel spoke. "I wonder what will befall the next unlucky guest, and who he or she will be," he remarked.

"Must you ruin my dinner by indulging in such morbid speculation?" Mr. Macmillan-Brown said irritably.

"I beg your pardon," Nigel said. "But that *is* the question on everyone's mind, isn't it?"

Hugh appeared through the pantry door to serve the appetizer. As everyone began eating, occasional murmurs of delight filled the room.

"It's lucky for the Petersons their food's so delicious," Malcolm said, eyeing his food happily.

"Good food makes up for a multitude of sins," Nigel pronounced as he leaned toward the girls' table. "I'm delighted to say that my dinner seems to be exactly what the menu advertised."

Once Nigel turned back to his meal, Nancy's eyes darted toward Malcolm. She quickly cast about in her mind for a tactful way to question him about the road sign. After learning that he had first arrived at Moorsea Manor only an hour before she and George had, Nancy asked, "Did you have any trouble driving into Lower Tidwell on your way here, by any chance?"

Malcolm's blue eyes narrowed. "Why do you ask?"

"Well," Nancy said innocently, "it's just that when George and I approached the village, the sign for the *B* road was missing and the *A* road sign was in the wrong place."

Malcolm blanched. "It was?" he croaked.

"Yes. You don't remember that?" Nancy asked.

"No," he whispered. "You must have been seeing things. I'm glad you're getting yourselves a holiday here—I'd say you both need a rest."

"We weren't seeing things, Malcolm," Nancy

declared. "That sign could have caused a really bad accident. George and I nearly rolled backward down the hill."

"Is that the honest truth?" Malcolm asked George suspiciously.

George nodded reluctantly.

Malcolm dropped his gaze, staring down at his half-eaten food as if he wished it would go away.

Nancy sat back in her chair and studied Malcolm as he nervously picked up his fork. There was one thing she was sure of: no one had framed him. He must have taken that road sign, she concluded, or else he wouldn't be acting so guilty.

After dinner Malcolm slipped upstairs, pleading a headache, while the other guests went into the living room. Georgina propped a book open on her lap and peered at it, birdlike, through tiny wire-rimmed reading glasses. The elder Macmillan-Browns and Nigel settled around the jigsaw puzzle, quarreling from time to time about where certain pieces fit. George, Nancy, and Ashley sat down to play hearts, but Nancy had a hard time focusing on her cards. Who could have taken Maisie? she wondered, glancing outside at the fog. I hope she's at least somewhere safe and warm on this damp, creepy night.

Sunlight streamed across Nancy's bed, waking her early the next morning. She sat forward as

George stepped out of the bathroom wrapped in a terrycloth robe, toweling her short wet hair.

"The fog's completely gone," George commented, "so Malcolm and I can play tennis. What's up with you today, Nan?"

Last night before bed, Nancy had briefly told her about the note on Maisie's collar. "I'm worried about Maisie," she said, "so I want to talk to Annabel about her, just in case she knows something I didn't learn last night. Then I'd like to question the Singh brothers—the developers Annabel told me about—and maybe look around for clues in their office, like a sheet of Moorsea stationery for Maisie's note or something about the treasure hunt. I was hoping you'd come with me, George—I might need help."

George smiled. "Sure, I'll come. Malcolm and I can always play tennis later. But would the Singhs be in their office on a Saturday?"

"Annabel told me they were realtors as well as developers," Nancy said. "And since they're in the business of showing people houses to buy or rent, I'll bet they work on Saturday."

As soon as Nancy had showered and dressed, she and George headed downstairs to breakfast. Malcolm had entered the dining room a step ahead of them.

"Hi, Malcolm," George said. "Are you up for some tennis later today?"

Malcolm's face fell when he saw the girls. "Oh . . . sure—but later," he mumbled. Then before George could answer, he sidled away from her and sat down between Nigel and Ashley at the far end of the main table.

The two girls sat down at the side table. "He's avoiding us," Nancy whispered.

"You're telling me," George said, her dark eyes flashing with annoyance.

"Maybe because we asked him about that sign," Nancy said. "He's obviously uncomfortable about it—like a guilty person would be."

"Yeah," George agreed in a defeated tone. Then she dug into her eggs in a brooding silence.

After breakfast, Nancy and George found Annabel in her office, looking pale and unhappy but determined to perform her duties as hostess of Moorsea Manor. After questioning her gently about Maisie's disappearance, the girls assured her they'd do everything they could to find Maisie, expose the culprit, and bring life at Moorsea Manor back to normal.

Annabel bit her lip and added, "That dog has known nothing but love all her life. I hate to think of her being at the mercy of someone who doesn't care about her—who might even mistreat her."

Nancy told Annabel they were going to check out the Singhs that morning. "Maybe we'll have a breakthrough and find Maisie," Nancy said hopefully, although privately she felt the chances of that happening at the Singhs' offices were very slim.

Fifteen minutes later, Nancy and George stepped out of their car in Lower Tidwell in front of the single, modern low-rise office building.

"Yuck," George commented as her eyes scanned the building. "This building could be in any American mall. It's hideous."

"That's for sure," Nancy said.

Inside the building, Nancy and George asked the receptionist whether the Singh brothers were around. "Yes," she answered, putting down her novel with a put-upon expression. "May I tell them who you are?"

Nancy and George introduced themselves and said they were interested in buying a house in the area.

"Really?" the receptionist asked, with a toss of her bleached blond hair. Then in a bored tone, she called Devendra Singh over her telephone intercom.

Several minutes later, a tall slim man in a white turban appeared. He wore a dark business suit with a bright green necktie.

After introducing himself, he led the girls down a corridor past several closed doors—offices, Nancy guessed. Entering a large corner office with a desk free of clutter, Nancy and

George were introduced to another man who was the spitting image of Devendra, except that he wore a red necktie instead of a green one.

"This is my brother, Rajiv," Devendra explained as they all shook hands.

"Dev and I are experts on real estate in different parts of the county," Rajiv said, squaring his shoulders proudly, "so if you girls tell us exactly where you'd like to look for a house, one of us will surely be able to help you."

"Actually," Nancy began, "my father, who's in the States, has been on the lookout for a large property to buy in England. George and I have been staying at Moorsea, and we heard a rumor that it might be for sale. If that's true, my dad might be interested in considering it." Nancy was fudging to see the brothers' reaction, but only a hint of surprise showed in Rajiv's eyes.

"That's odd," Devendra said. "I haven't heard of any such rumor. How about you, Raj?"

"No, and I must say I don't believe it," Rajiv answered. Turning toward Nancy and George, he explained, "Dev and I have approached the owners several times about buying the place, and each time they've firmly refused. If they do decide to sell, I believe they'd approach us first—they know we'd give them the best deal. We've made them a couple of extremely tempting offers already."

"Did you hear that rumor from another guest

at Moorsea?" Devendra asked. "Or from someone in town?"

"Oh, from another guest," Nancy said vaguely. "Someone has been playing these strange pranks at Moorsea lately, and I heard that the Petersons might be fed up with the responsiblity of running an inn."

"Pranks?" Devendra asked. His eyes flickered for an moment, as if he knew more than he was saying, Nancy thought. "Like what kind?"

"The Petersons' dog is missing, for one thing," George offered.

Rajiv studied the girls shrewdly for a moment, then said, "If you're so interested in the place, why not ask the Petersons about it directly? Why come to us?"

"Because if the rumor isn't true, they might be upset by it," Nancy explained. "Some people think that the prankster is harassing the Petersons so they'll lose business and be forced to sell."

"Ridiculous!" Devendra exclaimed.

"No one would harass the Petersons just to get Moorsea Manor," Devendra said scornfully. "That sounds like a Dartmoor ghost story— amusing to hear, but totally unfounded."

Nancy leaned forward on the desk, doing her best to scan it without seeming obvious. But other than a blotter, a notepad, and a quill pen, the desk was clear. Nancy sighed. There's no way

I'll be able to search the desk drawers with these guys watching, she thought. Better to try to sneak in some time when they're not here.

Nancy and George thanked the Singhs for their information. As the brothers led them back down the corridor toward the receptionist's desk, Nancy heard a noise coming from behind a closed door. It sounded like a dog whimpering. But what would a dog be doing in someone's office?

A sudden sharp yap made Nancy jump. Maisie? she wondered. Curious, she turned the doorknob.

10

Disaster on the Moor

Nancy opened the door, and a furry golden blur streaked past her. A golden retriever, Nancy saw. Catching up to the brothers, the dog leaped on them, whining excitedly.

The Singhs whirled around. "Why did you let Doone out?" Rajiv asked Nancy, his eyebrows drawing together in a single black line. "He's a total disruption to our office unless he's confined."

"You two have no business opening a closed door in our office," Devendra snapped. "I'm caring for my wife's dog today, and I don't want him to get all riled up. He's a nuisance as it is."

"I'm so sorry," Nancy said, trying her best to come up with an excuse on the spur of the

90

moment. "I . . . heard a dog in there. It sounded like he wanted to come out."

"It's not your business to let him out," Devendra said, glaring at her. His dark eyes narrowed with suspicion. "You thought Doone might be the Petersons' dog."

"No, I didn't, I promise," Nancy insisted. "It's just that I like dogs and he was whining. I should have asked your permission first."

"You certainly should have," Devendra said coldly. "We'll escort you to your car now, if you don't mind."

Once outside, Nancy and George made a beeline for their car. As Nancy was putting her key in the ignition, the brothers circled the car, one at Nancy's window and one at George's. Leaning against Nancy's door, Rajiv glared down at her. "We don't take kindly to being suspected of a crime, young lady. Never set foot on this property again or we'll call the police." He held his fist to her window, shaking it threateningly.

On their way back to Moorsea Manor, George put her hand to her forehead as if nursing a headache. "Whew, those guys were something," she exclaimed. "They kind of flew off the handle in a major way. And just because you let their dog out."

Nancy frowned. "They guessed we were there under false pretenses, and they were right. Still, I'm convinced they're hiding something."

"How can you tell?" George asked.

"Well, when we mentioned the pranks, Devendra's expression changed for a moment. It was as if he knew about them already and was worried we might find out. I was disappointed about one thing, though," Nancy added. "Those guys are too neat. There were no papers on their desk except for a notepad. Any clues would have been hidden away in the desk."

"And they sure weren't going to let you go through it," George said dryly. "I was racking my brain for a way to get them out of there for a minute, but I couldn't think of any excuse."

"Impossible. Those guys were guarding that office as if they were hoarding treasure in it." Nancy pulled the car into Moorsea's long drive. "By the way, George, how would you like to take a picnic lunch and ride out to the moors to look for Maisie?"

"Ride?" George said, perking up. "You mean, as in horses?"

"That's right," Nancy said with a grin. "The Petersons have those horses for guests to ride. Since Maisie doesn't seem to be inside the house or in any of the barns, my bet is she's off the property. The moors are huge, and Annabel said there are some high jagged rocks on them called tors. Someone could be hiding her in a cave in the tors." Nancy paused, then added, "Also, I'd like to check out Billy Tremain's house on the moor."

Once George and Nancy arrived at the house, they quickly changed into jodhpurs and boots. Then they headed downstairs to Annabel's office to tell her their plans. After giving the girls exact directions to Billy's cottage, Annabel warned them to stay on the path.

"Otherwise, the moors can be dangerous," she explained. "There are marshes and peat bogs that look exactly like solid ground—as George knows only too well. In fact, some people walked onto the moors and were never heard from again. And don't forget, even though it's a beautiful day now, fog can roll in without warning. And then you've really got to watch your step."

"What do we do if that happens?" George asked, glancing uneasily out the front window at the sparkling sunshine.

"Just stay where you are and wait for it to lift," Annabel said. "If you continue, you could easily lose sight of the path in the fog. And the horses are happy to stay still. They're smart animals, and they sense when there's danger."

"Could you do me a favor when I'm gone?" Nancy asked.

"Of course," Annabel said. "I'll do anything to help you find Maisie and solve this mischief."

Nancy smiled. "Could you, or the maid, bring me the small message pad that's in Malcolm's room? You know, the one with Moorsea Manor printed on it that comes with the room? I want to check the top sheet for indentations that the pen might have made in case he wrote Maisie's note."

"I'll take care of that straightaway," Annabel promised. "I hope you girls have a productive ride—and a safe one."

Half an hour later Nancy and George were picnicking in the shade of an ancient oak tree in the woods between the house and the moor. Nancy's chestnut mare, Foxfire, was grazing nearby while George's bay gelding nibbled a carrot she held in the palm of her hand.

"There's nothing like a British ploughman's lunch," Nancy said, finishing her sandwich. "English cheese with peasant bread and pickled onions—it definitely hits the spot."

"Well, Blue Moon sure appreciates his carrot," George commented. "But what do you say we head on? It might take us a while to get to Billy's farmhouse, especially if we're also searching the moor for Maisie."

Soon Nancy and George were back on their horses, with lunch leftovers stored in their saddlebags. The trail led out of the woods and onto the moor. Up close, the stark expanse of windswept hills covered with purple and gray heather was hauntingly beautiful. Unbroken by anything but occasional jagged rocks, like the teeth of some long-lost giant, the moor was strange and grim but somehow thrilling. A herd of wild ponies roamed around, their shaggy manes matted with mud.

As the girls followed the footpath, which wound through the heather, they scanned the moor for possible places Maisie could be hidden. But after searching several of the tors and finding nothing, Nancy began to feel discouraged.

The moor was vast. From Nancy's vantage point on Foxfire, it seemed limitless, like the night sky. Maisie could be in a zillion different places, and they'd never find her.

George trotted up alongside Nancy. "Don't you think we should have come to those rocks Annabel mentioned by now? You know—the landmark where the path forks toward Billy's?" she asked. "We've been riding over the moor for an hour, and Annabel said the rocks were forty minutes down the trail."

Nancy frowned. It was true. Annabel had mentioned a group of five gigantic rocks in a ring where the path forked. Nancy had seen no sign of them, and to make matters worse, the horizon behind them looked gray and fuzzy, unlike the crystal-clear landscape in front of them. Could the fog be rolling in? she wondered.

"Well, we spent a bunch of time checking the tors for Maisie," Nancy said. "That kind of messed up our forty-minute time frame."

"Hmm," George said, glancing to either side. "The light looks different suddenly. And I can't see the woods in back of us anymore. The hills all look the same. We might as well be at sea without any point to guide us."

"We've still got the path," Nancy said, forcing a smile. Her smile disappeared as she noticed the sudden weird purple-gray color of the sky—the same as the ground. Now, on all sides, she could no longer see the horizon.

"The fog's coming in for sure," George said grimly.

Out of nowhere, a gray, cottony fog and a relentless drizzle descended on the moor. Nancy couldn't believe the swift weather change. Fifteen minutes earlier, she could see for miles. Now, she could barely detect the path a foot in front of her. She looked around and her chest tightened—she could no longer see George.

"Nancy!" George yelled from somewhere behind her.

Foxfire leaped forward, shying at the sudden noise. Before Nancy could tighten the reins, the mare bolted across the moor. Nancy's heart leaped into her throat as they charged through the mist. She yanked on the reins, desperately trying to stop the crazed mare, expecting at any second to sink into a deadly bog.

11

A Figure in the Mist

Once more Nancy tugged on Foxfire's reins, struggling to stay on the horse. She couldn't tell whether they were still on the path, but she doubted it. The mare was in a total panic as she galloped frantically over the hills.

A man's figure loomed out of the fog, a dark silhouette in the grayness. Next to him was the shadowy form of a large dog. Nancy shivered. Who could he be, she wondered, roaming the moor in the rain and mist? He had the spectral appearance of a ghost, his features hidden by the fog.

The man suddenly put out his arms. He leaped toward Foxfire, trying his best to stop her. Foxfire darted away, and Nancy lost her balance. Nancy gripped the horse tighter with her thighs, trying to stop her slide.

"Foxfire!" the man cried. His voice was surprisingly gentle, as if he loved animals and was good at dealing with them.

At the sound of his voice Foxfire slowed her crazy run, and Nancy heaved herself upright into the saddle. She fought to take control. After a moment she did manage to calm the mare and finally bring her to a complete stop.

"Foxfire!" the man called again, coming closer. Nancy started, and her arms went limp with shock. As the man's features took shape from out of the fog, Nancy saw it was Billy Tremain with Maisie walking obediently by his side!

Billy grabbed Foxfire's reins and scowled up at Nancy. "What's the big idea riding through the moors in this fog?" he demanded roughly. Nancy gaped. His harsh voice sounded totally different from the one he'd used to cajole Foxfire. Maybe he was angry with her from their encounter in the sheep barn, but he showed no sign that he even recognized her.

"Don't you know the moor is dangerous in the fog?" he continued, his lip curling into a sneer. "You need to stay put till it moves off and you can see the trail again. Even I'm staying put till it lifts, and I've been familiar with this moor since childhood."

Nancy squared her shoulders. How dare the

guy talk to her as if she were a total idiot? "I know the moor is dangerous, but I had no choice," she said coldly. "Foxfire ran away with me."

Billy shot her a scathing look. "If you don't know how to handle Foxfire, then you shouldn't be riding her." He lovingly stroked the horse's neck. "She's an excellent mare who deserves an experienced rider."

A sudden chill ran through Nancy. Where was George? Between her efforts to control Foxfire and her surprise at seeing Billy, Nancy had been completely distracted. She hoped George had minded Annabel's instructions and stopped Blue Moon on the footpath.

"I'm with my friend, George," Nancy said to Billy. "We got separated when Foxfire ran away. I hope she's okay."

Holding Foxfire's reins tightly, Billy called out for George. Foxfire pranced in place at the sudden sound.

To Nancy's relief, George answered, not too far off. "Who's that?" she asked through the fog.

"Billy Tremain with your friend," he shouted.

"I'm okay, George. Are you?" Nancy yelled.

"A little spooked" came George's voice.

Billy warned George to stay where she was till the fog lifted. For a few moments Nancy and Billy waited together in an uncomfortable silence. He hunched down next to Maisie, while

Nancy sat nearby on Foxfire, who had grown completely relaxed in Billy's presence.

"Isn't that the Petersons' dog?" Nancy finally asked, searching for a tactful way to question him. After all, she reasoned, she was alone with him in the middle of a treacherous moor—she didn't want to anger him too much.

He shot her a suspicious look. "I take it you're a guest at Moorsea Manor—riding Foxfire and knowing Maisie here."

"That's right," Nancy said. "Did you know that Maisie has been missing since yesterday, and the Petersons are worried sick about her?"

Billy's eyes narrowed. "No, miss, I didn't. And now I suppose they'll suspect me of taking her. What really happened is I rescued her. But the Petersons never give me the benefit of the doubt," he added sullenly.

"You rescued her?" Nancy asked. "From where?"

"From a cave back there," he said, gesturing with his thumb in the direction behind him. "The poor thing was tied up inside the cave next to a trickle of water, but not a speck of food to be found."

"You just happened to go by that cave and you found her?" Nancy asked.

"Yes. I was taking a walk over the moor before the fog rolled in," he explained. "I heard cries coming from some nearby tors. I went to investigate, and found her just inside the mouth of the cave, unharmed but so lonely and hungry. It was enough to break a man's heart, it was." He reached over to pat Maisie, who gazed at him appreciatively through her white mop of hair. She did look a bit thinner, Nancy thought, under all that shaggy fur.

"And where were you taking Maisie just now?" Nancy asked.

"Why, back to Moorsea Manor, of course," he said rudely. "Where else? Her owners may not think much of me, but I know she misses them—I wanted to get her back there right away."

"Do you remember seeing me yesterday?" Nancy asked. "In the sheep barn at Moorsea?"

Billy shrugged. "I don't have much of a memory for humans. Don't put much stock in them. They're mostly the same to me, unlike animals." Then a sudden flicker of recognition appeared in his green eyes. "Ah, yes, I remember you now," he said. "You were that snippity girl who asked me who I was—as if I had to explain myself to you."

"But what were you doing in the barn?" Nancy asked, ignoring his confrontational tone.

"Because I love the sheep I took care of, and I miss them deeply," he said with a bitter edge to his voice. "They're my friends."

Nancy studied his face. Despite his surly manner, he seemed sincere.

In a faltering voice, he went on, "You see, a lamb died under my care. I should have realized the mother was having trouble with the birth, but I thought I could handle it. I got overconfident, and I didn't call the vet in time. One of the lambs was born fine, and the other . . . well." He stopped, and a shadow of guilt passed over his face.

"I heard about that lamb. I'm sorry," Nancy said gently.

"I felt so bad for the poor ewe. So I'll often sneak in to visit her and her little lamb—it makes me feel better, just being with them. And I think it makes her feel better, too. That's what I was doing when you found me yesterday, miss."

Nancy sighed. These didn't sound like the words of someone who would plot to destroy the Petersons through subtle, intricate tricks. After all, Billy seemed hardly able to distinguish one person from another. Would he really have known who Lord Calvert was, much less his parliamentary rival? Would he have known that Nigel Neathersfield was a food critic and then gone to the trouble of messing up his dinner? Most of all, she couldn't imagine him mistreating Maisie.

The more she thought about Billy, the less likely a suspect he seemed, which left the Singh brothers and Malcolm at the top of her list. As soon as she returned to Moorsea, she was determined to investigate the dog note.

"The fog's lifting," Billy commented.

Nancy looked around. Sure enough, she could see some large rocks about a hundred yards away that she hadn't been able to see before. She could also see the footpath, about fifteen feet to her right. "Well, that didn't take too long," Nancy said.

"The fog comes and goes around here," Billy said. "There's no predicting it." He headed for the footpath.

Nancy followed. "George!" she called out. "We're coming down the path. Stay where you are, and we'll find you."

Moments later Nancy and Billy found George sitting on Blue Moon about a hundred yards down the footpath.

"Hey, Nan," George said, grinning. "You're a sight for sore eyes. I was beginning to wonder if we'd be here all night." Then she suddenly gaped at Maisie. "Where'd you find her?" she asked in amazement.

Nancy introduced Billy and quickly explained how he'd found the dog. When she finished, she turned to Billy and asked, "Could you take us to the cave where you found Maisie? I'd like to hunt around it—maybe there's something there that could give us an idea of who took her."

103

Billy frowned. "She's a hungry girl, is Maisie. I want to get her home. But if you can find something that might point us to who took her, then I'm all for that. We don't want any more animals stolen and half-starved."

George cocked an eyebrow toward Billy. Nancy could tell she was surprised they were trusting one of their main suspects to guide them across the moor. Leaning toward her, Nancy whispered, "I think he's okay."

Ten minutes later Nancy, George, and Billy were standing outside a small cave, in a tor about fifty yards from the footpath. Billy pointed inside the cave to an iron ring stuck into the wall. "Maisie was tied up to that ring by a leash looped over her neck," he explained. "I've got the leash in my pocket now, though, since she follows me of her own free will."

Turning, he led the animals to a nearby rock where he waited for the girls. Except for a few stray wisps, the fog had disappeared. Once again, sunlight shone cheerfully on the moor.

Taking a flashlight from her saddlebag, Nancy began to search the back of the cave as George poked around near the front.

Something glittered in a corner. Stooping, Nancy picked up a shiny gold object near the trickle of water Billy had described. Holding the tiny object in the palm of her hand, she brought it into the patch of daylight at the mouth of the cave.

"Look, George," she said. "I found an earring." The girls peered down at the flat, square gold stud. "And there's a flower engraved on it—a morning glory."

George shot Nancy a baffled look. "Huh? Does this mean a woman took Maisie?"

12

Midnight Strikes

"We don't know for sure that a woman took Maisie," Nancy said.

"But the earring points in that direction," George said. "Which means we've had totally wrong suspects all along."

Billy's gruff voice interrupted them. "Come along now. It's already late afternoon. We shouldn't be lingering on the moor—and I've got a return trip to make, too." He poked his head through the cave and scowled.

"You're right, Billy," Nancy said, sticking the earring in the pocket of her jodhpurs. "It is getting late."

"If we start back to Moorsea Manor now, we should be safe enough," he added. "But the main thing is, I want Maisie fed, the poor, hungry, long-suffering thing."

Back at Moorsea Manor, the girls untacked their horses and rubbed them down. Once they were in their stalls, Billy took the leash from his pocket and looped it around Maisie's neck. Then he handed the dog to Nancy. "Please tell Mr. and Mrs. Peterson I found their dog," he said. "But I don't want to see them. They'll think *I* took her. Just make sure she gets a good meal," he added over his shoulder as he trudged away.

With Maisie on the leash, Nancy and George went to find Annabel and Hugh, who were working in their office.

Maisie bounded into the room, whining excitedly and jumping up and down, a mass of white whirling hair. The instant the Petersons saw her, they rushed over to her.

"Where'd you find her?" Annabel asked. She knelt on the floor near her dog and slid the leash off her neck.

Nancy briefly told the Petersons about running into Billy on the moor and discovering the earring in the cave. She also gave them Billy's account of why he'd been hanging around their barn, and she told them how well he behaved with animals. "He seemed so upset by the death of that little lamb," Nancy added. "I really don't think he's got anything to do with the stuff going on at Moorsea."

Annabel knit her brow as she listened, then shot a questioning look at Hugh. "I suppose we could always rehire him," she said with a rueful smile.

"Don't speak too soon, darling," Hugh declared. "If you ask me, Billy could still be guilty. He could have planted the earring in the cave and then rescued Maisie to make himself seem innocent."

"I think that's unlikely," Nancy said. "Billy seems to act on instinct. He's not the type to make a complicated plan like that."

"I wonder if the earring could belong to the wife of one of the Singhs," George remarked. "We know that Devendra, at least, has a wife. Her dog was at their office this morning."

"That's possible," Nancy said. "But it's also possible the earring has nothing to do with the case. Someone could have lost an earring in that cave before Maisie was even taken."

"Speaking of Maisie," Hugh cut in, "it's time for her dinner."

"And it's time for me to go help Peggy prepare our dinner," Annabel added. Flashing Nancy a dazzling smile, she said, "Now that Maisie's home, I feel much more optimistic about our case."

"One thing, Annabel, before you go," Nancy said. "Did you have any luck getting Malcolm's message pad?"

"Ah, yes." She reached into a desk drawer and pulled out the pad. Nancy examined it in the light of the window.

"I don't see anything," she said, before handing it back to Annabel.

"Well, girls," Annabel said, "we'll see you both at dinner."

After the Petersons left, Nancy said, "I know you don't agree with me, George, but Malcolm still looks guilty. I'd like to keep a close eye on him tonight. That road sign is pretty suspicious, and also nothing bad has happened to him at the inn so far. And just because there's no mark on his message pad proves nothing."

"But what about the earring, Nan?" George asked. "I know you said it might have nothing to do with the case, but I kind of doubt it. I mean, how many visitors does that cave get? It's in the middle of nowhere. I'll bet you anything the person we're looking for is a woman—or at least has an accomplice who's a woman, like Devendra's wife."

"Still, let's take turns watching Malcolm's stairway through the night. Who knows? We just might catch him getting ready to do some trick."

"All right," George agreed, "but I'm convinced you're suspecting an innocent man."

* * *

"I say, Annabel," Ashley Macmillan-Brown remarked over her lemon cake with mint-flavored sheep's milk ice cream that evening at dinner. "This dessert is scrumptious. I'd thought sheep's milk ice cream sounded foul, but really it's lovely."

Annabel smiled as she poured the guests coffee from a gleaming silver pot.

"This *is* good," Nigel agreed. "I'm so glad that the right food has managed to come my way for the last three nights. Maybe these strange pranks have ended."

Annabel laughed as she set the coffee pot down. "I hope so," she said, holding up crossed fingers. "Did everyone know that Maisie was found this afternoon? Perhaps that's a sign that our run of bad luck is finally over."

"Could be," Malcolm said cheerfully. "After all, nothing too awful has happened here since yesterday when Maisie disappeared—unless we count my embarrassing loss at tennis today to Nigel." He slapped the restaurant critic on the back as the man was sipping his coffee.

Nigel glowered at Malcolm. "Don't you dare do anything to compromise my perfect meal," he snapped, mopping up a spot of spilled coffee from his lap.

Mr. Macmillan-Brown cleared his throat. "Nothing awful has happened today, that's true," he mused. "But does that mean the pranks have ended? Or does it mean that the culprit will strike again soon, now that the dog has been found and everything *seems* to be back to normal?"

"But the Dartmoor area is never normal," Georgina put in. "No one expects it to be."

There was an awkward silence as everyone digested Georgina's remark. Then Nigel said, "Macmillan-Brown, you're making me nervous. Let's not dwell on bad things that might happen but probably won't."

"Has it occurred to anyone that the chap might be one of us?" Ashley asked innocently. Her worried eyes scanned the various guests.

"Hush, dear," her mother said. "That's a bit rude."

Everyone finished dinner in an edgy silence. Finally Malcolm pushed back his chair. "I'm tired—I think I'll read in my room this evening. I intend to get a good night's sleep so I can beat George in tennis tomorrow," he added, winking at her.

George shot him a pleased smile. "He doesn't seem to be annoyed with us anymore," she whispered to Nancy.

Nancy leaned toward George. "No, but if he thinks we're onto some other suspect, he's wrong," she murmured. "Let's go to bed early so we can watch his room."

After dinner Nancy and George sat around the living room fireplace for a while with the other guests and told them about their ride on the moor. After they'd described the fog coming in, Georgina gave a horrified gasp, then chimed in with yet another ghost story. When Ashley asked her father to play a game of chess, the group broke up to do different activities, and Nancy and George excused themselves to go upstairs.

Once inside their room, they cracked open their door, which had a perfect view of the third-floor stairway.

"This is a lucky break for us," Nancy commented. "We can watch Malcolm's stairway from our room. Do you want to take the first watch, George, or shall I?"

"I'll do it," George offered. "You get some shut-eye, Nancy. I'll wake you if I hear any action—human, ghost, or otherwise."

"Thanks, George," Nancy said with a grin. After throwing on a nightgown, she settled gratefully into bed. Within minutes, she was fast asleep.

"Nancy!" George's urgent voice woke her. "Someone's walking in the hallway!"

Nancy sat up with a jolt. She could tell that several hours had passed because the bright hallway light was off and a hush had fallen over the house.

In two seconds flat, Nancy joined George by the cracked-open door. The girls huddled down and peered through it. A small lamp in the downstairs foyer provided a dim light.

Soft footsteps padded nearby. Nancy held her breath, listening. To her surprise, the footsteps weren't coming from Malcolm's upstairs room. They were coming from down the hallway to their left.

"Maybe those stories about Dartmoor's ghosts are true," George whispered.

"No way, Fayne," Nancy muttered. "You're letting Dartmoor get to you." But despite her bold words, her spine prickled.

Of course there were no such things as ghosts, she told herself, but the big old silent house was creepy at this hour. She shivered, hugging her nightgown to her chest as she crouched by the door. She didn't dare open it wider for fear the person would notice them.

The grandfather clock in the downstairs foyer slowly began to chime, drowning out the sound of the footsteps. Twelve chimes, Nancy counted. Midnight.

Once more the footsteps sounded in the hall, and Nancy thought she heard a soft sigh. Could it be the wind? she wondered. She cast an anxious glance behind her at the curtain fluttering in the night breeze.

She looked again through the crack—and her breath stuck in her throat. In the shadowy light, a pale, eerie-looking figure glided into view. It was a woman wearing a long white robe, moving with her arms outstretched.

13

The Haunted Hallway

A rush of adrenaline shot through Nancy as the apparition floated by them. After the stories she'd heard about ghosts in Dartmoor, she couldn't help but feel shocked at the sight of one. After a moment Nancy took stock of the situation. The pale woman wasn't some specter roaming the halls of Moorsea Manor by night. She was Georgina Trevor—sleepwalking!

With her eyes closed, Georgina moved toward the large curved stairway that led downstairs. She started down it, her wraithlike shadow moving like some huge insect on the cream-colored wall. Seconds later she disappeared around a bend.

Nancy and George traded amazed glances.

115

"Let's go," Nancy whispered. She grabbed a robe from a hook on the door and threw it on.

They hurried into the hall. Clutching the banister, they peered down the stairs just in time to see Georgina's white robe trailing into the dining room.

Nancy and George ran down the stairs. Their bare feet made no sound on the cold marble floor of the foyer. They tiptoed into the dining room.

The pantry door was swinging back and forth, but the dining room was empty. "She's in the pantry," Nancy whispered, pointing at the door.

"She seems to know exactly where she's going," George commented suspiciously as the two girls sneaked toward the door. "Wouldn't sleepwalkers be acting a little klutzier? I'll bet she's faking."

"I'm not sure," Nancy said. "Let's open the door and see what she's doing now."

George opened the pantry door a crack and peeked through. Turning to Nancy, she said, "Georgina's in there, all right—standing totally still in the kitchen doorway. I can see the back of her robe."

"I wonder if she's tampering with tomorrow's breakfast," Nancy said. "Hurry. Let's follow her." Hustling past George, she pushed the pantry door open wider. A sudden gut-wrenching squeak from the hinges made goosebumps rise on Nancy's skin and made George jump.

Georgina whirled around. "Who's there?" she screeched, her watery eyes wide with shock. "Oh, it's you two. You gave me a fright. I thought you might be one of the ghosts that live in this house." She placed a hand on her heart, breathing heavily.

"We're sorry, Georgina," Nancy said, pretending to be surprised at seeing her. Fudging an excuse so that Georgina wouldn't think they'd followed her on purpose, Nancy added, "Uh . . . we couldn't sleep, so we decided to come downstairs to get a snack."

"You say there are ghosts here?" George interrupted. "Have you seen them?"

"No," Georgina said with a dismissive shrug. "But I'm certain they're here—somewhere. I can feel it in my bones."

"So, what are you doing here, Georgina?" Nancy cut in. "Looking for a snack, too?"

Georgina wrinkled her tiny nose, reminding Nancy of a confused rabbit. "A snack?" she echoed. "No, I don't think so. I must have been sleepwalking. I do that from time to time. In fact"—she glanced around with a puzzled air— "I have no memory of coming down here at all."

"You were wide-awake when we walked through this door," Nancy remarked.

"Was I? Well, that awful squeak must have woken me up. The Petersons really should oil that hinge. It's disgraceful."

"The Petersons have had a lot on their mind, lately," George said.

"Ah, yes," Georgina said with a vague smile. "They have, haven't they?"

Nancy studied Georgina as the older woman gazed into the distance. Was she really this, absentminded and weird? Nancy wondered. Or was she putting on an act? One thing Nancy was sure of: no way was she going to leave Georgina alone and go back to bed.

Nancy stepped forward and slipped her arm through Georgina's. "Let's go upstairs. George and I want to make sure you get to your room safely."

Georgina fluttered her eyelashes. "Don't worry about me, Nancy. Why don't you girls fix yourselves snacks? I can get back upstairs on my own just fine now that I'm awake."

"No," George said, taking her other arm, "we insist. You still seem a little shaky. We can't let you go back to your room all alone."

Georgina looped her arm through George's. Then, bowing her head, she meekly allowed herself to be escorted upstairs to her room.

"I must have had a bad dream," she murmured along the way. "That's usually why I sleepwalk."

"All these ghosts in the house," George said, arching an eyebrow at Nancy over Georgina's head. "They make it impossible for anyone to get a good night's sleep."

Georgina beamed. "You're an understanding soul," she commented once they'd reached her bedroom door. She looked George over approvingly. "Those spirits do make it very hard for one to get a good night's sleep." Then, without another word, she flitted into her room and shut the door.

Nancy and George hurried back to their room. Once inside, Nancy said, "So, George—do you think it's possible for *anyone* to be that spacey? Or do you think she's covering up a clever plan to tamper with our breakfast?"

George burst out laughing. "Sorry, Nan," she said after a moment. "But I've been stifling that ever since Georgina opened her mouth downstairs. That stuff about the ghosts is too much. I can't figure her out at all. She doesn't seem capable of putting together a single straight sentence, much less masterminding a plan to put the Petersons out of business."

Nancy thought about the earring she had found in the cave. Could it be Georgina's? she wondered. "Tomorrow," she said aloud, "I'm going to search Georgina's room. If I can find the matching earring, then our mystery will be solved." Sneaking a grin at George, Nancy added, "Sorry to disappoint you, George, but Malcolm isn't off the hook—he might still make an appearance. Anyway, you go to sleep. It's my turn to watch."

By five in the morning, Nancy had slipped back into bed in frustration. After their midnight encounter with Georgina, the house had been disappointingly quiet.

"She's sick?" Nancy asked, staring in surprise at Annabel the next morning. "What's wrong?"

Nancy, Annabel, and Hugh were standing on the beach. The Petersons were cleaning rowboats and securing oars in the locks, preparing for an exploration party to a nearby island later that afternoon.

The crisp sea breeze slapped against Nancy's face. Sunlight danced on the blue water, and tiny whitecaps foamed here and there across the huge expanse of sea. The crescent-shaped beach, littered with driftwood and shells, was sheltered, but the waves looked bigger today than they had before, Nancy thought. Hugh was taking a quick break from his work to throw sticks into the sea for Maisie.

"Georgina's got a headache," Annabel explained, responding to Nancy's question. "She came down to the kitchen early this morning and told me she felt quite under the weather, so I fixed her a breakfast tray, which she took upstairs."

"I guess there's no way I can check out her room this morning," Nancy said, feeling frustrated.

Annabel shook her head. "I'm sorry, Nancy, but Georgina's definitely up there. She told me she hopes to sleep off her headache after breakfast, and she asked that the maid wait till the afternoon to clean her room. Apparently, Georgina didn't have a very good sleep last night."

Nancy cast her mind back to the unsettling events of the night before, but she decided not to bother Annabel with them now. Nancy had wondered why Georgina hadn't appeared at breakfast—and decided it was probably because she'd slept late after her nighttime wanderings.

Annabel turned her hazel eyes on Nancy. "By the way, Nancy, I hope this case isn't getting to you. After all, this is supposed to be a vacation."

"Don't worry about me," Nancy assured her. "I'd rather be doing something about the case than sit by and watch all this stuff happen."

"Well, I hope you'll take the afternoon off and join us for the boating party," Annabel said.

Nancy gave her a thumbs-up sign. "Count on me for that, Annabel."

Nancy walked back up the wooden stairs to the bottom of the lawn at Moorsea Manor. From the top of the stairs, Nancy was reminded of what a magnificent place it was. With its stately stone facade gleaming in the sunlight and ivy spilling over its ancient eaves, the house was breathtaking. Nancy clenched her fists in determination—she *had* to get to the bottom of this mystery and save Moorsea for the Petersons. She couldn't let Annabel lose her ancestral home.

"Nancy, lass," a man's voice shouted. Turning, she saw Malcolm and George strolling toward her from the small parking area next to the house. "What a beautiful day," Malcolm exclaimed. "I was about to take my wee bairn out for a spin with George when I spotted you on the lawn. We were hoping that you would join us."

"Your wee bairn?" Nancy said as they joined her.

"My baby. My brand-new convertible Jaguar. It's my prize possession. All it needs is a couple of pretty lasses riding inside." He flashed the two girls his signature grin.

"Come on, Nancy," George urged. "You should see Malcolm's car. It's really something. It'd be a hoot to take a ride in it."

"We'll see some nice views of the sea," Malcolm said. "With the wind in your face and the sun sparkling—what better way to pass the morning?"

Well, I *would* like to ask Malcolm more questions, Nancy thought, studying the playful gleam in his eye. She felt a sudden wave of irritation toward him. Was his humorous personality for real? she wondered. Or was it a cover for something darker? "I'd love to come," she said, and they headed off for his car.

Ten minutes later Nancy was clutching the

backseat of Malcolm's cherry-red Jaguar as he floored it around hairpin curves. Inches away from the car, enormous cliffs plunged down to the rocky shore thirty feet below. From the front passenger seat, George glanced nervously back at Nancy. Cupping her hand to her mouth, George muttered, "I wish he'd stop showing off. We're going to end up impaled on those rocks below."

Nancy nodded grimly. Why was Malcolm driving like such a hotrodder? she wondered. Was he trying to scare them off the case?

Nancy's knuckles were white as she gripped the seat and leaned toward Malcolm. "Slow down!" she shouted, but the sound of her voice was drowned out by the wind.

Soon, the houses of Lower Tidwell appeared, zooming into sight like a movie in fast motion. Malcolm would have to slow down now, Nancy realized.

They proceeded down the main street with Malcolm hunched over the steering wheel, clucking about a slow car ahead. He slapped his thigh, then said, "That car is going at a snail's pace. Do they think I have all day?"

On Nancy's left, the stark office building of the Singh brothers came into view. Nancy was surprised to see both men standing outside their front door on a Sunday. They were probably showing houses to a client, she reasoned, catching sight of a third person behind them. Suddenly one of the Singh brothers shifted his weight to the side, and Nancy gaped. The third person was Georgina Trevor!

George and Nancy traded alarmed glances. Georgina must have driven into town when Nancy and the Petersons were down at the beach.

"Malcolm!" Nancy said, tapping his shoulder. She had to get back to Moorsea Manor right away to search Georgina's room. "Can you turn around? Immediately?"

"Turn around?" Malcolm asked. His face was filled with disappointment as he craned his neck toward Nancy. "You don't mean it! Why?"

"I need to get back to Moorsea Manor." Nancy fumbled for an excuse. "I . . . uh, I'm expecting a transatlantic call in five minutes. Do you think your 'wee bairn' is up to the job of getting us there in time?"

"Of course she's up to it," Malcolm replied in a sullen tone. "The question is whether she wants to be."

"Come on, Malcolm," George urged. "Be a good lad and drive us home."

"Okay," Malcolm said glumly. "If you insist."

Back at Moorsea Manor, Malcolm skidded into his parking space with a loud crunch of gravel. Then without a word to the girls, he jumped out of the Jaguar and slammed his door. By the time Nancy and George stepped out, Malcolm was already jogging briskly up the front steps of the house.

"What's his problem?" George wondered with a puzzled frown.

"I guess he's insulted because a phone call is more important to us than a car ride with him," Nancy said. "Maybe he wanted us to ooh and aah over his car more."

"That's very grown-up of him," George said dryly.

"Do I detect a slight change of opinion over Mr. Malcolm Bruce?" Nancy asked with a sly grin. She punched George playfully on the arm as they hurried to the Petersons' office to fetch Georgina's room key.

Nancy pulled George to a sudden stop just in front of Reception. Running footsteps clicked loudly on the stairway above them. Nancy and George whirled around. Whoever was running sounded frantic, Nancy thought.

Malcolm appeared, ashen-faced, at the top of the stairs. "There's a snake—coiled in my bathroom sink!" he gasped. "A huge black snake!"

14

Swept to Sea

Annabel rushed out of Reception, joining Nancy and George at the base of the stairs.

"What's all this commotion?" she asked, glancing from Nancy to George.

"I'm afraid I'm the cause of it," Malcolm said as he descended the stairs.

Annabel paled. "Why? What happened, Malcolm?"

In a shaky voice, Malcolm told Annabel about the snake. The moment he had finished, she bounded up the stairs, two at a time, with Nancy, George, and Malcolm on her heels.

Up in Malcolm's bathroom, Annabel, Nancy, and George peered cautiously at the snake. It was about three feet long, curled up placidly in the

126

sink as if it lived there. "Whew—it's just a garden snake," Annabel proclaimed. "Completely harmless. I'm going to ask Hugh to remove it." With a little shudder, she left the room.

Nancy turned to Malcolm, feeling puzzled. He really did seem shaken by the snake, she thought. She doubted he was pretending. Then what was he doing with the sign in his closet if he wasn't reponsible for the other pranks? "Malcolm," she began, "I thought I'd let you know what I found the other day." She opened his closet door and pointed inside.

Malcolm's jaw dropped, and then a hurt look came into his eyes. "You were snooping in my closet?"

"I'm a detective, Malcolm," Nancy explained. "The Petersons wanted me to get to the bottom of all these weird things that were happening at the inn, so they let me search some guest rooms for clues. We thought the sign might be another trick. Remember when I said that George and I almost slid backward down that hill?"

"I didn't mean for that to happen, really!" Malcolm said in an anguished voice. Then he clamped a hand over his mouth. "I can't talk about this anymore."

"Would you like to talk to the police, then?" Nancy asked.

"No," Malcolm said, his blue eyes widening. "Okay, I'll tell you then." In a sheepish tone, he explained, "I was driving my Jag a bit too fast the day I arrived at Moorsea. I ran into the road signs, side by side at the fork in the road. I knocked them down—by mistake, of course—and then I must have stuck the *A* sign back where the *B* sign belonged. But I didn't realize my error, I promise!"

"But why did you take the *B* sign and hide it in your closet?" George asked.

Malcolm's face turned red, and he refused to meet George's eyes. In a stricken tone, he said, "I was in a hurry—I just wanted to get away. I was about to stick the *B* sign back when I heard a car approaching. I didn't want to get caught, you see—bad publicity, and all"—he flashed George an embarrassed glance—"so I threw the sign in the back of my Jag. I know I did wrong, and I meant to replace the sign, but with you two lovely girls around, I just forgot." He sneaked a hopeful grin at George.

"Yeah, right, blame it on us," George muttered, rolling her eyes.

Nancy studied Malcolm. He certainly was kind of silly, she thought, but his story sounded true. In any case, she doubted whether someone so impulsive and easily distracted could have planned the pranks and the dognapping. What could Malcolm's motive be, anyway? More and more, Georgina, the Singhs, or the three of them together seemed the likeliest suspects. And even though Nancy couldn't figure out a motive for Georgina, she *was* acting awfully suspicious.

"All right, Malcolm. I believe you," Nancy said. "But tell me, had you locked your bedroom door this morning?"

"Yes," Malcolm answered. "I can't understand how anyone got in."

Nancy drew George aside and said, "I've got to search Georgina's room."

"I'll keep Malcolm company till Hugh arrives," George offered.

Nancy found Annabel in the kitchen telling Hugh about the snake. As soon as she finished, he grabbed a large paper bag and a pair of thick work gloves and hurried out of the room. Nancy pulled Annabel into the pantry, away from the kitchen staff, who were busy preparing lunch.

Nancy filled Annabel in about Georgina's recent activities—the sleepwalking, talking to the Singhs, and lying about staying in her room to nurse a headache. "It's possible that after the treasure hunt, Georgina lied about getting a clue that sent her to the roof," Nancy declared. "I wonder if anyone actually saw Georgina slipping on the roof and hurting her ankle."

"I certainly didn't," Annabel said. "And I doubt other guests saw her, because they were busy following their own clues."

"I'm wondering if she could be in league with the Singhs," Nancy said. "See, the twins could have hired Georgina to do the pranks. After all, they wouldn't want to be seen trespassing at Moorsea because they'd instantly be suspected, but Georgina as a guest would have free run of the place."

Annabel looked thoughtful. "That makes sense, Nancy, except that Georgina seems so . . ."

"Clueless?" Nancy finished. "It's kind of hard to tell whether she's putting on an act or whether she's really that spacey. Anyway, I'd really like to search her room. If I can find the matching earring, we'll be in luck."

Annabel led the way back to her office. As she pulled Georgina's extra key off the peg board behind her desk, Nancy noticed that the key to Room Seven was missing.

"Hey—Georgina could have sneaked in here this morning and taken Malcolm's extra key," she remarked, pointing at the empty peg. "Maybe she forgot to put it back after leaving the snake in his sink."

Annabel did a double take as she noticed the missing key. "You're right. Georgina, or . . . whoever, probably took that key."

With Georgina's room key in hand, Nancy hustled upstairs. The house was entirely still. All the guests were probably outside enjoying the beautiful weather before lunch, she reasoned.

Quickly—aware that Georgina might return at

any minute—Nancy slipped inside the room. She made a beeline for the bureau. A makeup kit sat on top of it, with a heart-shaped papier-mâché jewelry box nearby. Inside the jewelry box were a few pairs of earrings.

A thrill went through Nancy. Nestled among them was a single gold stud, identical to the one she had found inside the cave!

Nancy put the earring in her pocket and hurried downstairs to find Annabel. In Reception Annabel was sorting through some old photographs and organizing them into an album. She raised her eyebrows when Nancy showed her the matching earring. "So Georgina is our villain," she said, shaking her head in amazement. "I guess now we should contact the police and show them this earring as proof."

"It's just one piece of evidence, Annabel," Nancy countered. "It's not total proof. Before calling the police, I'd like to catch Georgina doing one of her pranks. If the police question her now, she'll be on her guard. Also, we still don't know whether she or the Singhs are the masterminds. I don't want the Singhs to be alerted so they can cover their tracks."

Annabel sighed. "All right, Nancy. As usual, I trust your judgment." She picked up a photo of a dapper-looking couple and their young daughter to place inside her album.

"Who are they?" Nancy asked curiously.

"This is me with my parents when I was six," Annabel explained. Cupping her chin in her hand, Annabel gazed at the picture dreamily. "My parents look happy here, but I know it was a tough time for them. My sister, Gloria, had run away from home the year before. She never came back, and everyone assumed she was dead."

"She ran away?" Nancy asked, surprised. "That's so sad. But . . . how old was she then?"

"Gloria was twelve years older than me, so she was seventeen when she left home. She was completely wild—the black sheep of the family. I remember her fighting constantly with Mum and Dad. Then suddenly she was gone."

"Why did she fight with them?" Nancy asked.

"No one really knows," Annabel replied. "My parents were good people—loving and not too strict. Gloria was just one of those types who could never be satisfied, no matter how much anyone tried to accommodate her. At least, that's what Mum said. Still, she blamed herself for Gloria's problems."

"Why?" Nancy asked.

"Because when Gloria was three, Mum and Dad moved to India for two years for Dad's job. They left Gloria in England with Mum's sister. Even though Gloria resented my parents and fought with them, Dad absolutely doted on her. He used to call her his 'little morning glory.'"

"His 'little morning glory?'" Nancy repeated.

She held up the earring between her thumb and forefinger, studying the etching of the morning glory on the flat gold surface of the stud. "Do you have any pictures of Gloria?" Nancy asked, eagerly scanning the pile of pictures.

"No," Annabel answered. "My poor parents were so heartbroken after Gloria left that they threw out her pictures in a fit of grief. Whenever Mum looked at those pictures, they made her cry. My parents decided they'd best get on with their lives for my sake."

Nancy held out the earring for Annabel to see. "Do you remember whether Gloria owned a pair of earrings like these?" she asked.

Taking the earring from Nancy, Annabel examined it with a puzzled frown. "No, I don't remember. Why?"

"I could be wildly off base," Nancy said, "but I'm wondering if Georgina Trevor and Gloria Trevellyan are one and the same."

Annabel's jaw dropped. "Georgina? Gloria?" she said, aghast. "What makes you think so?"

"Well, this is a small thing and maybe a coincidence, but the earring has a morning glory on it, which fits with Gloria's nickname," Nancy explained. "Also, Georgina is probably in her early to mid-forties—about twelve years older than you. And it makes sense that the villain would be familiar with this place—she, or he, would have an easier time organizing the pranks."

"Yes, like knowing about the dumbwaiter in the pantry that no one ever uses," Annabel said. "I'll bet that's where she hid Nigel's meat loaf until she had a chance to switch it with his real order."

Nancy shot Annabel a smile. "Also, come to think of it, you and Georgina look a little alike," she said carefully. "The red hair and small noses."

"Dear me," Annabel said, looking alarmed.

Just then, something outside the window caught Nancy's eye. It was Georgina—sneaking through some underbrush on the far side of the lawn and heading toward the cliff above the beach. Moments later she disappeared down the cliffside stairs.

Nancy jumped up. "Annabel, I just saw Georgina. She's on her way to the beach."

Annabel swiveled around in her chair to look outside. "What in the world is she up to?"

"There's no telling," Nancy said. "She might be sneaking down there to do something to the boats for the party later. She was acting pretty suspicious—sneaking through the underbrush instead of walking across the lawn. She definitely didn't want to be seen."

"Nancy, really, I'd be happier if we called the police," Annabel said. Her hand shook as she picked up the phone.

"Not yet," Nancy said. "Let me follow Georgina first. As I said, if I can catch her in the act, we'll have proof that she's the person we're looking for.''

Annabel looked at Nancy hesitantly. "Okay, Nancy,'' she said, "but please be careful. If Georgina's capable of sending guests into quicksand and beehives, she's obviously dangerous. I don't like the idea of your being alone with her. In fact, I'd like to find Hugh to back you up.''

"Okay,'' Nancy said, "but I'm heading down to the beach this minute. If I don't hurry, I might miss her in action.''

Nancy cut through the dining room and out the kitchen door. She raced across the lawn toward the channel, skimming over the grass like a deer. At the top of the stairs, she paused, looking down at the sea. Even though the day was clear, the winds had picked up since morning. Waves swelled on the choppy water.

Rushing down the stairs, Nancy scanned the beach for Georgina. She was nowhere in sight. A sudden gust of wind swirled up sand, stinging Nancy's eyes. She shielded her face in the crook of her arm.

The breeze died for a moment, and Nancy looked up. Four rowboats were pulled up on the beach near a large rock, all set for the exploration party. Nancy rushed over and glanced inside them. No Georgina.

She climbed into the nearest boat, curious to

see if she could find any evidence of sabotage. Hunching over, she inspected the hull.

The rowboat suddenly lurched, and Nancy stumbled backward and landed on the bottom of the boat. But before she could figure out what was going on, the rowboat started to slide across the sand toward the sea!

Nancy lay on her back, thrown off balance by the jerky movements of the boat as the waves slapped against it. She struggled up onto her elbows.

Peering over the stern of the boat was Georgina, her face full of grim determination. "Good riddance to you, Nancy Drew," Georgina cackled as she gave the boat one final push. "You're going out to sea now, and no one will be the wiser!"

The strong current took hold of the boat, and Georgina waded back toward shore. As the choppy waters buffeted it, Nancy sat up, grabbing for the oars.

Her heart sank. The oars that Annabel and Hugh had attached earlier were gone! Georgina must have taken them, Nancy realized. She sat up helplessly in the boat as the current swept it out to sea.

15

Strong Swimmers

Nancy glanced around the boat. Other than a bailing bucket and a rope coiled in the prow, it was empty.

She peered out to sea. Nothing but the horizon lay ahead, but on her right was a series of rocks that led into shore. Once more, her gaze darted to the rope. Her mind clicked away.

If I can loop the rope onto one of those rocks, she thought, then I can use the other rocks as stepping-stones to shore. She bit her lip. Her idea was a long shot, she realized. The waves were rocking the boat like crazy; even if her aim was good enough to lasso a rock, the rope might not hold on to its slippery surface.

What other choice did she have? She picked

up the rope and quickly knotted a loop. The rocks were getting closer—close enough for the rope to reach them, she judged.

Nancy waved the rope around in the air to get the feel of it, like a cowboy preparing to lasso a steer. Then, without wasting another moment, she hurled it toward the nearest rock.

The rope missed, falling in a limp circle in the churning water. Adrenaline pumped through her as she drew it in. The current was pushing the boat away from the rocks. If she didn't catch the rock this time, she wouldn't get another chance.

Nancy gritted her teeth, trying to estimate the distance between the boat and the rock. Once more, she took aim. Whirling the rope in a circle above her, she fixed her gaze on the jagged point of the rock.

She threw the rope, holding her breath as it sailed through the air. To her amazement, it caught the rock, looping around its middle. She yanked it tight. For one heart-stopping moment, the rope slipped up the rock toward the top. Her jaw clenched. Was it going to hold? she wondered.

Nancy let the rope slacken for a moment, then carefully tugged it. This time, she felt a resistance, as if she had just caught a fish. She let out a long breath of relief. She'd hooked the rock!

Hand over hand, Nancy hauled the boat closer

to the rock. Waves bashed the hull as it collided with the huge boulder.

Leaning into the rock, she tightened the rope, doing her best to keep steady. If she could just pull herself onto it without getting smashed by the waves, she thought.

Nancy threw her arms around the rock. Hugging it for dear life, she dropped the rope and clambered out of the boat. Instantly, the current swept the boat away.

Waves crashed around her legs as she struggled to lift herself higher onto the rock. Barnacles tore at her hands. She sneaked a look down at the swirling surf. If she let go of the rock now, she'd be dashed against it—or else sucked out to sea.

With an enormous effort of will, Nancy strained to lift herself onto the rock. Her sneakers gained a toehold against the barnacles, and a moment later, she was up. Doubled over, she gasped for breath as she stood precariously on top of the boulder.

Something moved ahead of her. Nancy jolted upright, just in time to see Georgina standing in a row boat, brandishing an oar. Aiming at Nancy's shoulders, Georgina made a wicked swipe through the air.

Nancy ducked in the nick of time, and the oar passed harmlessly over her head. She's trying to knock me back into the water! Nancy realized. Nancy raised her head. "Gloria Trevellyan!" she cried, standing up straight and fixing Gloria with a penetrating stare. "Put down your oar!"

Gloria froze. Her colorless eyes were pinpricks of hatred as she glared at Nancy.

"You've been trying to drive the Petersons out of business to benefit the Singhs," Nancy declared. "I'm guessing they'll give you a share of the profits if they develop the land—or something like that. I bet they realized you'd be happy to help them because you're jealous that Annabel owns your parents' estate. I'm onto your game, Gloria, so you might as well give up now."

For a split second Gloria stared at Nancy. Then she burst into high-pitched peals of laughter— an eerie, hollow sound half-muffled by the wind. "The Singhs had nothing to do with my plot," she proclaimed. "I only hoped they'd want Moorsea badly enough to help me out, but no such luck."

Nancy hesitated, surprised. "So you asked them for help with *your* plan, instead of the other way around?"

"Yes, and they refused me," Gloria told her. "After you caught me in the kitchen last night, I worried that you might begin to suspect me. So this morning, I went to them for help."

Nancy stared at Gloria. What could her motive be in sabotaging Moorsea Manor if the Singhs weren't paying her? she wondered. Was it simply her resentment that Annabel owned it? Gloria's pranks seemed like a great deal of trouble and risk to make up only for that reason.

"I can't believe you went to all this trouble just to get revenge on Annabel for owning the place," Nancy said.

"I'm tired of all this talk," Gloria sputtered. "I'm afraid you'll never get to know my full story." Once more Gloria raised her oar, her boat teetering slightly. With an evil gleam in her eye, she lowered her oar again.

"Gloria," Nancy began, her shoulders squared. "Annabel is onto you. She went to alert the police. It's just a matter of minutes before you'll be arrested."

"Liar! You're bluffing just to save your skin," Gloria cried.

"It's the truth," Nancy said evenly. "The police are on their way. So far, you haven't hurt anyone seriously, Gloria, so the courts might be lenient with you. You don't want to make things worse for yourself."

"You think you're so smart, Nancy Drew," Gloria spat out. "Well, here's what I think of you and your clever detective work." With a sudden whoosh, she lifted her oar and swiped it at Nancy.

Nancy ducked—a moment too late. With a violent whack, the oar butted Nancy's shoulder, knocking her into the sea.

Waves lashed at Nancy, buffeting her mercilessly against the rock. She struggled to keep her head above the waves. Choking on a mouthful of seawater, she reached for the rock, desperately trying to get a grip on its slippery surface.

But the current was too strong. No matter how hard she tried to hold on to the rock, the tide swept her farther and farther out. Even though Nancy was a strong swimmer, she knew that in minutes she'd be in the open channel with the land receding from view. Her body might as well have been a piece of seaweed or driftwood for all the control she had in the powerful surf.

More seawater poured down her throat as she fought to stay afloat. Coughing, she flailed with her arms—and suddenly touched something firm. She glanced to the right. A pair of black eyes stared up at her from under a wet mop of hair. Maisie!

Making loud snuffling noises, Maisie swam up next to Nancy. Nancy flung her arms around the dog, hoping she'd be strong enough to help her swim.

With the waves slapping against their faces, Maisie paddled through the churning sea, buoying Nancy up the whole way back to shore.

Nancy straggled up on the beach. Water poured off her T-shirt and shorts. Maisie shook herself, sending drops of water flying. Out of the corner of her eye, Nancy saw Gloria jumping onto the beach from her boat.

Annabel, Hugh, and George were rushing down the wooden stairs. "Hold it right there, Gloria!" Hugh shouted. "The police are on their way."

Gloria froze.

"The game is up, Gloria," Annabel said, staring at her sister as if she were seeing her for the first time. She shook her head. "What ever made you do this?" she breathed.

"As if you'd have to ask," Gloria hissed.

Annabel sighed. "You must have discovered the terms of our parents' wills."

"That's right—through public access to the documents," Gloria replied. "I learned that they left you everything."

"Not exactly," Annabel countered. "First of all, they thought you were dead—they hadn't heard from you for over twenty years. Naturally, they left Moorsea Manor to me."

"Naturally!" Gloria snapped.

Annabel went on. "But they stipulated that if I

143

ever sold Moorsea and you showed up within a year after the sale, then you and I would split the money. They knew you could find out the terms of the will easily enough. Since you hadn't even bothered to tell them whether you were alive or dead, I'd say their will was pretty generous to you."

"Generous!" Gloria said. "That's what you think. What if you had never sold Moorsea? I would have been left out in the cold, with nothing."

"But I would have let you live at Moorsea with me. I don't see it as mine—I see it as belonging to all the Trevellyans. Dad wanted to keep Moorsea in the family. He would have been thrilled to have both of us living here."

Gloria sneered. "How sweet of you to offer."

"But why plan an elaborate sabotage that hurt people?" Annabel went on in a pained voice. "Why didn't you just come to me and tell me who you were? It's because you never cared about Moorsea anyway. All you ever wanted was the money. You were trying to bankrupt my business so I'd be forced to sell."

"Speaking of the sabotage," George cut in, "how did you manage to substitute your fake clues for Annabel's clues at the treasure hunt?"

"That was easy," Gloria said, chortling at the memory. "I knew that Annabel had hidden her

144

clues a few hours before the hunt began, and she kept everyone's first clue in the top drawer of the dining room sideboard—I watched her put them there. So I followed a few of the leads and substituted some of my own clues. Creative, weren't they?"

"Works of art," George said dryly.

"What about the danger sign that had been on the gate to the beehives?" Nancy asked. "What'd you do with that?"

"I tore it off and stuck it under a nearby rock," Gloria told her. "And just in case you're still wondering, it was *I* who threw the bronze horse from the upstairs window before ducking back into my room." She paused, scowling. "I had to scoot under my bed when Annabel rudely burst in."

"And what about the snake?" Nancy asked. "Is he some sort of pet?"

"No, only a lucky find. I was strolling in the garden early this morning and noticed him curled up inside an empty watering can." Gloria wrinkled her nose. "But I had to stay in my room with that creature all morning till I got a chance to plant him in Malcolm's sink."

Just then four police officers ran down the wooden stairs, brandishing wooden clubs.

"You can put your clubs away, gentlemen," Gloria said, raising her arms in surrender. "My sister here has won her war." Then she offered each arm to an officer as if they were escorts at a ball and allowed them to lead her quietly away.

There was a long moment of silence. Overhead, a gull cried. Waves slapped against the wet sand. Taking a deep breath, Annabel murmured, "Even though Gloria's going to jail and won't be plaguing me at Moorsea, my life will never be the same. I have a sister now."

"Yes," Nancy said. "In one morning, your whole life has changed."

Once more everyone was silent, taking stock of the case. Then Nancy told Hugh, Annabel, and George that the Singhs had nothing to do with Gloria's plot.

"There's one thing I don't get," George said. "If Gloria approached them this morning for help, why were they acting so weird when we questioned them yesterday about the sabotage? It was almost as if they knew something about it."

"I thought so, too, at the time," Nancy replied. "But I think they reacted that way because they were happy to hear about the pranks. They probably thought it was great news that someone was trying to force a sale, but, of course, they didn't want to let us know they felt that way."

"The Singhs weren't totally innocent, though," George said. "Since Gloria had told them about her scheme this morning, they should have warned Hugh and Annabel about it. But they didn't because they realized they'd benefit if it did work out."

Maisie trotted over to Annabel with a piece of driftwood in her jaws. Shaking her head around playfully, she let Annabel remove the stick and then throw it down the beach for her.

"Maisie sure is an awesome swimmer," Nancy commented, watching the dog retrieve the stick.

"Well, she's used to these waters," Annabel explained. "She plays in the channel all the time and knows where the currents are and how to get out of them. She may be a puppy at heart, but she's basically full-grown—a big dog now. She could pull someone your size to safety, Nancy, as long as you weren't too far from shore."

"Well, if it hadn't been for Maisie running ahead of you guys," Nancy said, patting the bouncing dog on the top of her shaggy head, "I'd be out to sea by now."

Annabel shot Nancy a grateful smile as she tossed the stick again. "And if it hadn't been for you, Nancy Drew, I'd be out of business. Thank you so much for solving this case."

"Now Moorsea Manor can continue as before," George said, smiling. "Successful beyond your wildest dreams, Annabel."

Hugh smiled. "Let's forget the boat party for today, everyone. The sea is way too rough."

"We'll have a celebration up at the house instead," Annabel suggested happily. "An indoor treasure hunt this time—and tea."

"So what's the prize if we win?" Nancy asked.

"A mystery-free holiday," Annabel said, and grinned.